Chesapeake Bay Stories

Raymond McAlwee

Printed in the United States of America

Fourth Printing 2014

© 2009 by Raymond McAlwee

Tanner Press

P.O. Box 650321

Potomac Falls, Virginia

20165-0321

ISBN 978-0-615-32666-5

Library of Congress Catalog Number in Publication data

This is a work of fiction. All names and characters in these stories are products of the author's imagination. Except for 9/11/2001, all other dates, characters and events are used fictionally.

Book design by Denise McDonald

Contents

Acknowledgements

W.A. Dorrance, 1904-1998, Author, Guggenheim Fellow
for Fiction, Professor Emeritus, Georgetown University
Doctor, you not only taught me how to write but how to read.

The Lost Dog and Cat Rescue Foundation
www.lostdogrescue.org

High praise for:

Jessica Lovelace, Artist
www.jessicalovelacestudios.com

Denise McDonald, Book Designer
denise.mcdonald@comcast.net

DEDICATION

For Whitey Schmidt,
my friend and hero of the Chesapeake Bay.

For all the loyal, dedicated and hard working
team members of Mona Electric, please accept
an autographed copy of "Chesapeake Bay
Stories" by Raymond McAlwee. Ray's uncle,
Bob McAlwee was the business agent for
local# 26 and helped Cap to obtain work as a
union apprentice and later find key personnel
for the fledgling company as Mona Electric
began to grow. Bob's son Marty, is Ray's first
cousin and Cap's great friend from St. John's
High School. Ray is also the editor of "Mona
50th Anniversary" which may be found at
www.CapMona.com

"The Woodwind"

J.Lovelace

Illustrations by Jessica Lovelace
www.jessicalovelacestudios.com

PREFACE

When Captain John Smith made his discoveries of the Chesapeake's rivers four hundred years ago, his log conveyed the amazing experiences he and his party encountered. The Native Americans, some hostile, some hospitable, astonished him if only because of the nonchalance they held for the great bodies of unspoiled waters they inhabited. As a man of the ocean from an island nation burgeoning forth as a naval power since England's defeat of the Spanish Armada twenty one years earlier, the abundant natural beauty, breadth and wealth of the Bay heightened the spirit of exploration he'd known since crossing the Atlantic. His excursions took him up the Nanticoke to that fine river's headwater in Delaware and up the Potomac to what is now Georgetown where the rocky crags and shallow water prevented farther penetration. The Patapsco knew his boat.

Smith was an adventurer, the first governor of Jamestown, a rabble rouser, a hustler and by almost all accounts, the first author of fiction using the Bay and its tributaries as his settings. That Pocahontas threw herself on his tied-up, prone body at the last second before he was to be beaten to death by Powhatan Braves whose chief was her father, is a story line most writers, including this one, would be proud to have authored. Having that plot snatched from my fictional repertoire, I attempt to humbly follow in the captain's legendary prose. Some have suggested only the smallest parts of his history/fiction in his logs are true. The remainder comes from the fervid imagination of a writer who promoted its veracity to serve his own purposes, grew tired of mapping or thought it would just make a good story. *Chesapeake Bay Stories* fall into the last category. Writers are told to write partly what they know about; the remainder should be imparted to make the prose readable, enjoyable and rather curious and interesting. Unlike Smith, these stories will not succeed for four centuries. Like him in many other ways, they are set around the Bay and are works of fiction. The captain never returned to the Bay but did explore our northeastern coast and named it New England.

Raymond McAlwee
Kent Island, Maryland

A Chesapeake Sonnet

Forgive the past, soothe hurt, bypass dreads
Direct mighty energy to the common goal; Restoration
So our Chesapeake may be alive again with Oyster Beds
And let the Blue Crab regenerate its peak population

No to the poisons from the farm that foul the beach
Eschew the toxins of development that mar our shore
Then join together especially the young to strive and reach
The needed knowledge and habits to protect and restore

Only then industrious watermen may earn a rightful living
To supply overabundant delicacies we've come to miss
So then the boaters of pleasure will join in thanksgiving
For the joy of being on clean open water that gives such bliss

What has begun will succeed in triumph and forever allay
Today's problems and so help us all, we will Save the Bay

R. M.

SOLOMONS' WIDOW

Bob Hansbrough had grown up in Indianapolis, lettered in three sports for three years in high school, won a football scholarship to Notre Dame but instead chose an appointment to the U.S. Naval Academy. His father had a penchant for the peninsula in upper Michigan where the family owned a cabin on four hundred acres of waterfront property and vacationed every summer. Bob and his two older sisters loved the place as much as their parents. The kids took to the water naturally, swam like eels and could sail their skiff so well that their father had been encouraged to acquire a second larger sail boat to broker peace among his children. Because of more experience his sisters were better sailors but that gap narrowed as he grew older. Save for the marriage of the older girl, Mr. Hansbrough would have been put upon for yet a third vessel. Bob had never travelled east of Ohio except on a class trip which took them to Philadelphia and Washington D.C. The Academy overwhelmed him at first but with confidence and a pleasant smile adaptation came easier by Christmas. The work suited him and he survived as a Plebe without incident but not without questions. By the end of his first year an intrinsic calm came to him that said that he would and could do better job of leadership when called upon as an upperclassman. In his senior year the slightest of heart abnormalities almost prevented him from being assigned to flight school in Pensacola, Florida. No Navy doctor wanted to sign-off on an ensign who later might crash a seven million dollar plane into the stern or propellers of a carrier but they didn't reckon with the young officer's resolve and the esteem his superiors held for him. The doctors put Bob through every possible medical test and examination, even a series at Johns Hopkins, a heretofore rare exercise by the Navy. His commanding officers wanted Bob and, to a point, were willing to allow him to continue to pursue his career in naval aviation. With all the results calculated and evaluated, he left Bethesda Naval Hospital after a month in late June with an overwhelming clean bill of health and required no more physicals than his fellow officers.

He joined three other grads that weekend, his good friends at The Academy, at the summer home of the parents of the fiancé of one of the men. A week's vacation, relaxation and good-byes were the agenda. The house, located on the St. Mary's side of the Patuxent, led down to a pier with a nice sized sloop and was two miles down and across river from the sleepy little town of Solomons Island and the Bay. The four would be separated soon, scattered around the globe as was usually the situation. All four intended to remain in the Navy after their mandatory tour. They believed their service to be valuable to the country, the Navy and themselves. 1967 had brought more serious conflict than ever and as seniors they had been tutored on the strategy of the Navy as well as anyone knew it at the time; language, survival, and geography classes had been intensified to an extreme. The additional emphasis had actually been added to the main curriculum some years earlier.

No one at the outdoor bar they mingled in that afternoon could mistake the origin of the four. They stood out. No bartender, bouncer or saloon owner need have any misgivings about their behavior. If any untoward situation would have ever presented itself, everyone else knew that the young men would comport themselves with aplomb, tact and restraint. They were officers and gentlemen. The people along the Bay knew the reputations of the Academy and its students neither of which, within recent memory, had been besmirched. The fiancé had invited three of her friends to join them on a beautiful late Friday afternoon but only two came. The third had been delayed because her father needed to work late in Washington, and the family wouldn't arrive from Chevy Chase until later in the evening. The two other girls, college juniors, were known to all four and had been to Annapolis on a social occasion earlier that year. They had dated Bob's other two friends once. The future pilot had not been out with many young women since high school not because the opportunities hadn't presented themselves but because no one of particular interest had held any persuasion over him for very long, or indeed, even at first. His lankiness and confident stride betrayed his true height which was all of six feet. He looked taller. Scandinavian good looks caught most women's attention. He played football and lacrosse and studied with the passion he knew it would take to insure the successes he had guaranteed himself. By seven-thirty they were about to shove off in the sloop that had sailed them over from the western shore of that fine river when the third girl came running down the pier to the public dock where they had tied up. The women called to her to hurry while laughing and shouting her name, "Come on Evelyn."

She slowed her pace when she saw that the four professional sailors had cut the small engine and grappled the dock pulling the obedient boat back to its moorings. Taking off a pair of low heeled backless sandals she boarded with a hand from Bob. He held her hand a second too long for any extra unneeded assistance after she came on board and before he could help it, he became a little flushed and threw her hand out of his which worsened his already reddened condition. He had become at twenty-two a picture of self-possession and sang-froid; until, that is, that moment of embarrassment and he felt it too. After the smiley greetings were punctuated by compulsory hugs, Bob and Evelyn were the last to be introduced. They grasped hands for the second time and he had regained enough composure to mention perfunctory salutations.

"Can you take me down the creek? I've got a little one mast. You all could tow it over to the house and I'll sail or putt back home later. We just live over on the point," she said.

"You sail?" Bob asked.

"Yes I do and rather better than you played Army last year."

"Do you mean the team or me?"

"I meant the team but now that you mention it."

"Are you always so brassy?"

"Are you always so condescending?"

"I apologize. Both my sisters are beautiful sailors, handy, safe and fearless if need be."

"Do you mean they're beautiful women or beautiful sailors?"

"Both, boy, you're quick with ambiguities. Where do you go to school?"

"Boy?! Why do you assume I'm in school? I just finished my freshman year at UNC. Let me go change while you rig a line to her and we'll start over when I get back," she said, laughingly this time.

As they rounded the point close to where the Bay and river meet she jumped ashore, ran the sixty yards of wide, sprawling lawn to the house which had bountiful prospects of both bodies of water. The girl's sculptured but soft features and smiling but sexy green eyes encouraged a bout of gazing from which he knew he must desist when she returned. The home brightened the small promontory upon which it sat and made for a warm beacon. Across the water, the lights glimmered from the Patuxent Naval Air Station. The thousand stars that night shone down on the mouth of the historical waterway and illuminated the water in a way she had never witnessed; which would include her whole life. Tying her dark hair back she looked curiously at him all the way across; now her turn at resisting to stare. By the time they tied up across the river she and Bob couldn't hear anything the others were saying.

"My friends and family call me Evie."

"They called you Evelyn from the boat."

"They were chastising me for being late. They wanted me to meet you. Didn't you know? I almost didn't come."

"No, but I'm glad you did."

Later that night Bob and Evie held hands, kissed and promised to write. They kept in touch every day for four years, married, were stationed to San Diego and had a daughter. When Bob's ailment finally forced him to be grounded after three distinguished combat tours, he resigned his commission.

After little discussion he and Evie, who was pregnant again, moved back to Maryland and the Bay where he had left adolescence for manhood and more importantly, where they had met. He cared deeply for the region and it had been a large part of his wife's life since she could remember.

At first they lived in a rented house on the South River near Edgewater, so Bob could attend Maryland Law up in Baltimore. They wanted to be on the water. Their second daughter was born after a few months there. He opened a small office in the house from which to sell insurance, real estate, prepare tax returns and offer investment counsel. He studied, tested and became licensed for these ancillary occupations while he wasn't busy with the job of studying and passing the Maryland bar and rearing a young family. The bar exam presented no impediments to him, as he knew it wouldn't. The school geared its courses to that end and if anyone wanted legal theory they were often told to try Harvard.

Evie's parents still owned the house on the point but as her mother had been ailing lately they stayed at home near Washington and came less frequently. Her father offered to give them a rental property they owned on three acres, five doors and a mile up the point but the young couple insisted on paying full market value. Her parents more than admired Bob for his correctness in all matters but they loved him dearly for being the ideal husband to their only child and perfect father to their grandchildren. He was more than the son they never had. He had made that confident and happy family even more content than they ever thought possible. He was a good guy who was always smiling.

Bob renovated and added on to the house, opened his law

practice down that peninsula and hired solid young people to run and work in his insurance, real estate, brokerage and accounting businesses which he eventually also moved down to Calvert County. Their daughters, whom Bob tried to name Coral and Leyte, caused Evie some genuine concern. She remained resolute at each birth and held an insistent belief that the girls would be better off in later life or even at school if they weren't named after famous naval battles, no matter how feminine and historic. She prevailed. They settled on Laura and Mary, Bob's sisters' names.

Bob stood for the House of Delegates when the girls reached school age and defeated an incumbent old war horse to the disbelief and dismay of his own party. He had always been competitive and gravitated to the sense of duty. Refusing to run again after two terms, he encountered some enmity and vitriol from the party who began to flaunt him as the new young face of their slate. After a few terms in Annapolis he learned something about himself that he should have known. Politics can be a dirty game and the longer a delegate or state senator held office the more ingrained and tougher they had to remain. He would not impute any illegalities, as far as he could tell, but the turgid speeches, histrionics and the altogether disingenuous atmosphere of the place helped his decision. Everything to them was always and forever about money which is as it had been throughout history. The session was only a few months long. Each member needed to serve those who helped them into office. Once elected, they had to perpetuate, seek and curry the favor of the party leaders, swap their votes often for laws in which they didn't believe and be cajoled or vaguely threatened by lobbyists; this left time for little else. He resigned to the absolute bewilderment of his colleagues whose notion was, 'once you're in, it's time to cash in.'

Just by surviving in the House, his public reputation would be known and his private law practice promised to increase four fold at least. They couldn't fathom his decision since they held some prescient idea that he would serve in either chamber for twenty years; or even a higher office. He wanted to preserve his somewhat archaic idea of principle and honesty and simply couldn't justify continuing to represent with no true passion.

"Resigning your seat, are you a fool? What are you playing at? Is this your idea of scrounging up votes for some 'pork' I don't know about? You won't get my 'yea' unless you know what it'll cost you."

The author of this scurrilous diatribe was offered, only half kiddingly, by his bumptious neighbor in the next desk on the floor of the Assembly. The hardened politico had been rumored to be worth a hundred million dollars but was a jovial yet lonely old bachelor who wore the same shirt three days a week and wished his life away hungering for the next general assembly eight months hence. The codger's greatest joy was the rare call for a special session in the fall. He held only two political tenets; for capital punishment and against tax relief for low income workers. In time, Bob, thought he could have made a difference but that would have included remaining in politics.

The family prospered and the children grew to be as beautiful as their mother. They looked like twins and at almost seventeen and eighteen resembled Evie closely enough in bearing and appearance that they were often asked if they were all sisters. Their mother delighted in that question while the sisters feigned to be unhappy with the reference. The girls had an ally in Bob. With a wink and a nod to them he would alleviate some punishment placed on them by their mother. Of course they adored him for this; Evie not so much. If any rancor would ever be noticed in that home, it derived from Bob taking the girls crabbing or sailing when under restriction for some girlish trespasses usually unexplained to him because of his gender. If only one had committed some venial crime against propriety, Bob would sail the condemned one up to Chesapeake Beach to eat crabs at Abner's. Naturally, Evie saw his behavior as callow and undermining but the girls always related to her their father's reminder to them of how much they all loved each other and how one acted reflected on all. These little sermons never lasted more than two minutes. His amen was, 'always do the right thing.'

"Why do you reward them while I'm trying to discipline them?" Evie often asked.

"I just try to reason with them. They're great kids. We're lucky," he'd say.

"They've got you tied around their little fingers."

"I hope so."

Bob and Evie knew how much love they shared yet never spoke of it. Words for it were not only insufficient, they didn't exist.

By the time both girls married, the Hansbroughs were in semi-retirement and happy that both had chosen well. Laura remained close in Washington where her husband attended law school and she taught. Not Mary; Evie had seen this coming for a long time. She married an Academy man, not an aviator, but according to Bob, a bridge officer who had captain or admiral written all over him. Evie wondered if fatherly infatuation had a bearing on Mary's choice but then realized that her older girl married a law student. Bob liked and approved of both men and Evie knew that he knew. By the time they became blessed with grandchildren, twin boys for Laura and a girl from Mary, they had begun to sail the Chesapeake from Baltimore to Norfolk. A large coterie of good friends inhabited both shore lines and they received in Solomons by sail as many as they called upon. Visits to and from the girls were frequent and, unlike them both, they fell into the poor custom of so luxuriantly spoiling the three grandchildren as to suffer mild rebukes from their mothers. Once alone though, they set off on the forty-six footer Bob had given her on her fiftieth birthday.

"So where's my present?" she asked at the time.

Many of Bob's former classmates, even ones he hadn't known or were ahead or behind his class lived up some creek, harbor, inlet or water off the Bay. Added to that were friends he and Evie had made over the years and her friends from childhood. They lived on the boat whenever they visited. She contained all the comforts of home and he never missed a ball game, she, Masterpiece Theater.

To resupply their wine cellar at home and on the boat, a sail to their wine merchant in Annapolis treated Bob more than Evie to the naval tradition of provisioning in port. They would make the excursion last at least a week. The drive to the vintner from home would only take less than an hour and that included stopping for gas which they never seemed to have in either car but so it happened. If they could sail their beloved Chesapeake, they travelled on the water. Returning under sail to Solomons made the trip more worth the homecoming.

For their thirtieth wedding anniversary they sailed to England on the QE 2 round trip instead of flying home as most travelers opted for on that leg. For a pilot's wife Evie disliked flying especially when sailing or the train were an option. Cruises were an anathema to them both and they had never been on one. They eschewed London, rented a car and traveled to the west country of Dorset, Devon and Cornwall, always within sight or easy reach of the Channel and Atlantic. Bob received a special invitation to visit The Royal Naval College at Portsmouth from an expatriate and Academy man who taught there. The wives shopped in Chichester. The invitation also included being guests on the couple's yacht for two days to view the spectacle of Cowes Week off The Isle of Wight, the largest sailing regatta in the world; a fervent aspiration of theirs since retirement began to loom.

On their way, they kept to the more remote coastal towns by day and pub crawled in early evening in fishing villages where they talked on even terms with the locals about the sea. The fishermen had rarely met 'Yanks', much less ones like Bob and Evie who, not on purpose, created more good will than a crop of junior diplomats and attachés serving in Great Britain to that end. On the southerly route back passing The Maritime Provinces of Canada, the great liner caught the eastern edge of a weakening hurricane and for thirty-six hours the couple relished the stormy conditions of the ocean, conditions in which would have never found them on the water otherwise.

During the time away, their home, their life and their waters were never far from their thoughts. Financially sound, even rich by some standards, they led a less luxurious life than contemporaries of the same station. They ate sensibly and drank very good, well made vintage wines, but never to excess. The only extravagance they allowed themselves and were unable to check took place when a day at home called for household chores, maintenance and cleaning but if a breezy beautiful morning promised, it found them exploring St. Jerome's Creek over in St. Mary's or some other cove they'd last sailed to ten years ago.

After the Army-Navy game that year, in early December, Bob reluctantly prepared the cobalt hulled yacht for dry dock. He slowly took her up the creek listening for any nonexistent flaw that he would have corrected by the first day of spring. Evie had driven to pick him up. By the time she arrived, Bob had died. The EMTs were still on board. He had passed away suddenly on deck before she came out of the water. It was an untimely and unbearable death.

The funeral procession of cars and pedestrians had been as long as anyone could remember. Evie had done more comforting than accepting regrets and bore the tragedy to her family with resolve and grace unknown to and incapable of most. During the viewings Laura and Mary busied themselves as best they could but at the service and cemetery they trembled and sobbed with such abject grief that their husbands were unable to console them.

Evie made no attempt at blocking out the reminders caused by vast numbers of inanimate objects. They not only reminded her of Bob but she allowed herself hours and weeks of musings about the conversations, events and celebrations which had occasioned them. Naturally he lived in her heart, he always had. While he had busied himself at work, she held him constantly in her thoughts to alert, remind, cajole, or slightly admonish him about all the family matters in their daily life. Visits to the kids exacerbated rather than eased her disquiet. While they attempted to keep her mind off the recent past, they were living recollections of their father and all three grandchildren favored him. After a year she developed certain foibles that she considered unworthy of herself; sleeping later, drinking alone, working out less and inventing excuses at invitations. Bob had sold a small plane a week after Mary wed. Now she considered selling the boat. She'd get a small sloop, something she could handle easily alone but after two years the boat remained in dry dock and she'd been on the water seldom. The shock had eroded as her love for Bob remained as constant as when he was still alive. She rerouted the daily routine of her personal habits and functioned better because of it. She met friends for dinner, drove up to Deale and Galesville with them to eat crabs at Skipper's Pier or dine on the deck at Pirate's Cove and began to drink moderately again. She accepted a position as a substitute teacher especially if she were needed for English.

By the end of the summer she prepared to return to part time teaching, accepted an offer of travel with her friends to sail the Caribbean from Martinique that next winter and kept Jimmy Buffet's music on at home and in the car more than she realized. She had spent two weeks in San Diego while her son-in-law was deployed at sea and two weeks in Bethany Beach with Laura and her family. On the Saturday before Labor Day she reluctantly accepted an invitation to a wine tasting and dinner for about thirty, a number in which she felt comfortably obscure. That number had easily been surpassed by the time she arrived which made her feel better still. She unobtrusively offered three bottles of Le Montrachet to her hosts, the same couple who had introduced her to Bob all those years ago. No fear of being 'set up' or introduced to someone who 'has been dying to meet you' by these special friends, caused her any anxiety and prompted her decision to attend. They now lived on the Calvert shore closer to her and across and farther down river from the spot of that fateful night. They had recently bought the property after retiring and selling their home in Arlington, Virginia. More than half of the guests seemed paired while the rest were equally divided.

Evie didn't join in the tasting but did decide on a glass of the Montrachet with her friend surreptitiously on a separate deck off the large kitchen.

"Evie, this reminds me when we used to hide behind the boat shed and smoke."

"Yes, it was exciting because we hoped your brother and his friends would find us. They never did. Probably why we quit smoking; it's just as well."

"Well let's hope no one comes out here. I'd hate to share this; it is so good. Why don't we finish the bottle? You can spend the night."

"You and Ed come over one night and we'll sit out on the lawn. Besides I don't want you drinking any of that seven, eight-nine plunk they've brought. Drink this 'til you run out. I've got cases."

"By the sound of the party they should be on the fourth or fifth tasting by now. That's good, I'll be hardly missed. Have you noticed the very tall man in the UCLA tennis shirt? We met him last week at a 'Restore the Bay' conference in Annapolis. He's a marine environmental specialist from California for some new consultant group the E.P.A. just hired. He's very intelligent. Would you like to meet him?"

"No, and why from California, how can he help?"

"Oh Evie, you're always so pragmatic and questioning. We should take all the help we can get. By the way, there is a little piece of dirty work going on. The office manager at our bank has been after me to fix her up with someone. I didn't know anyone who would be her type. She's early thirties, divorced, no kids. Ed, in all his worldly wisdom, invited this guy who works in his father's boat yard where they're overhauling Ed's project, better known as 'Noah's Lark.' He's her age and good looking enough with a Calvin Klein ad body but in a blue collar, redneck sort of way; but even I could have picked someone better than him. He did bring two nice bottles of Chardonnay and a nosegay from the grocery store but he just told me he doesn't drink wine. Who comes to a wine tasting that doesn't drink wine?"

"Maybe he came for the bank manager."

"I don't think so. He doesn't know yet. I'm about to introduce them."

"What does she look like?"

"A lot less demure than she does at the bank; light brown hair with platinum highlights and a showgirl figure."

Inside, Evie circled the buffet hoping to find some of her friend's delicious crab balls. There were plenty and still warm. In fact, they weren't balls at all. When queried at times by party or dinner guests for her recipe for the smaller version of crab cakes, Joan would smile and offer, 'Oh, for four, just two pounds of jumbo lump, a couple of egg yokes, two big table spoons of mayonnaise and mustard, and bread crumbs. Don't forget to use good bread crumbs.' What she rarely mentioned was that she made her own crumbs with fresh baked toasted multi grain and rye breads and picked the crab meat fresh as soon as the 'Jimmies' were cool enough from the pot. She would then gently turn the lush white meat in the recipe with her fingers ever so slowly so as not to 'bruise' the lumps. By delicately pulling small gobs of the mixture out of the wooden mixing bowl with her finger tips, each 'ball' resembled a cross between a jumbo Hershey Kiss and a loosely crumpled-up dollar bill. Like snow flakes, no two had ever looked exactly the same. A sprinkle of JO spice on top of each creation finalized the prep. Observed in the broiler until that golden tan appeared, the aroma told Joan when they were done. She didn't know exactly how many minutes it took. That too, had probably never been exactly the same. Tooth picks carrying little nautical flags were inserted as a utensil. She served the creations in three blown glass crab boats which she had commissioned for that very dish. No one could entertain like her and Ed. Wine had become a new adventure for most of their friends over the last twenty years and she was glad for it. Pairing food with wine had united them even more than ever in retirement. She and Bob had only ever drunk wine; white in warm months, red in cold months and both when the true season could not be determined; or whatever a dish demanded.

She lingered and watched the now more animated and livelier guests. Evie had dressed in a straight khaki skirt and a white long sleeved linen blouse with rolled up sleeves. She wore the same make up she would wear to the governor's mansion or a crab feast. Espying a sandy blonde in front of four men who were attempting and failing at wit and impression, Evie couldn't help be struck that the woman was very attractive. However, more of Evie's attention drew itself to the white sun dress cut too low at the bosom and too short at the hem. The dress held itself up with thin spaghetti straps tied behind her neck. However, firm, large breasts made the straps redundant. Lilac Nike swooshes accented the dress front and back and her make up, daubed, lined, brushed and glossed on, coordinated to the color in the swooshes. Matching shoes with heels too high and thin made for precarious trips to the planked deck surrounding the house. When Evie did meet her in the kitchen she seemed genuinely pleasant and nice. She wore a redolent scent of lavender slightly too strong and musky since it pierced a room which held the wonderful aroma of crab balls and spiced shrimp. When asked by a gushing would-be lothario the shade of her ensemble, the banker described the color as 'sort of a new off plum Iris.' Among themselves later, the other women decided the color to be purple.

Evie did introduce herself to the Californian who had come this far to help in the effort to protect and preserve her precious Bay. She thought it good to let him know how much everyone in her community solidly backed the Bay's health and regeneration.

"What do you think your first initiatives will be?" she asked.

"Well the next two years should be spent re-examining the scientific and business model of the data collected to date, some of which I am very suspicious. Then a plan should be cautiously initiated so that it is agreeable to the watermen, business men, merchant ships, farmers and government. Your problems have many sources and few solutions."

"But haven't we already identified the causes? Surely it's the time for some action. A few of the ideas we've agreed to implement sound feasible and have shown good results lately. The crab population was up this summer and promises next year. Some ideas haven't, like the oriental oyster beds. I think the time for the studies and research should always be in progress but what's wrong with proceeding with the work now? It can't hurt."

"I've spent my life studying these matters. I do see your point but I'm the expert here. Twelve years in the laboratory and my PHD give me a somewhat decided balance when it comes to ecological and environmental opinions on our country's waterways."

"Do you ever go out on the water?"

Before he answered, he looked over Evie's head to the now tipsy, Lenten colored bank manager whose audience had almost doubled and he wished it would soon include him.

"No, I rarely stray out of the lab; I have people who do that for me."

"So you've never been on the Chesapeake?"

"No, if they extend my contract after two years, which I hope they do with a raise of course, I'll venture out one day if the weather's fine. Excuse me, time for a refill."

The phrase she searched for eluded her. Since she couldn't locate a mild expletive condemnation in her brain for this turgid creep, under her breath she settled for what was really on her mind; 'pompous ass.'

As she passed the group of hopeful losers and their temptress in plum, she heard the randy fop from the west coast slurping up to her, "Now where exactly is your branch? I'm unhappy with the bank I was recommended to and I may consider giving you my business."

'Oh,' Evie thought, 'I bet you would like to give her your business.'

She now sought out her friend for that second glass of the crisp, clear, French Chardonnay. She felt she needed and deserved it. Not finding either, she went to the seventy-two unit wine fridge they kept in the pantry and opened another bottle.

The sun had just fallen across the river when she took a turn around the deck to that side of the house to gaze at the river and other bank where her adult life had begun. Instead of finding her friend she came upon a young man who hadn't heard her approach and she slightly startled him.

"Oh, I apologize. Am I disturbing you? Are you O.K.?"

"I'm swell. No, I'd been watching the sun set. I guess I got lost in the moment," he said.

"Well I can't think of better reason for feeling 'swell' than watching that beautiful sight, especially this time of year when it sets a little farther south in a darker sky."

"Sounds like you've seen your share," he said.

"I've probably seen more than you."

"No, gee, I didn't mean it like that."

"I know."

"My name is Evelyn but everyone calls me Evie."

"My name is Frankie and that's all anybody's ever called me."

They both laughed at his attempt more at being friendly than funny. His drawn out vowels, slurred consonants, original intonation and pitch told her that he had lived in southern Maryland his whole life. She liked the accent and what it had represented; hard work on the farm or the water. Evie enjoyed speaking with him. She thought him nice. She decided to offer more.

"Ed and his wife are dear friends of mine. They introduced me to my husband. He passed away almost three years ago and I can't imagine how I would have held up without them. She told me she thought you worked for your father."

"She mentioned me? I feel she thinks I'm a little rough around the edges. My father is refurbishing an old wooden hulled sloop for Ed. He comes over to the yard a lot to help and my father lets him do some things, but nothing too difficult. Ed is pretty handy though and I can tell he's a real good sailor."

"He should be. He's a retired navy captain and an Academy man."

"Stands out a mile, you can tell those guys just by looking at them. I think about how good it is to have them on our side every time I see one, young or old."

As Evie started to reply she found no breath to form a word and a slight gasp escaped before she regained herself. His words, so simply put, moved and weakened her as she thought of Bob.

"So, you help your father at the boat yard. Are you helping him with Ed's boat?" She asked such an inane question only for time to compose herself more but it wasn't working.

"My father's retired too. He's just working with Ed because that antique is such a challenge."

"So, exactly what do you do?" Another feckless question which she had already asked, when was she going to make herself stop doing this?

"I'm a boat builder. I build boats. My father used to and he passed it on down to me."

"I must apologize again. I have to know. Are you building anything now?" she asked.

"Yeah, today we had a crane come in to turn the hull over on seventy-six footer. It's like topping out an office building but instead of putting up a fir tree the boys fly a 'Budweiser' flag on top of an old wooden mast from the Civil War. She'll be ready to launch soon but the owner doesn't want her 'til spring to sail her down to Jupiter, Florida, but we'll put her in the water soon and see if she floats."

"You mean you don't know?"

"That's the scary part, you never know until she doesn't sink."

She couldn't remember when she had been so interested in something or was it someone. This conversation had broken some kind of spell. She became enthralled and decided against the self-imposed ban she had put on more questions.

"What would a boat like that cost?"

"Quite a lot. I can't tell you how much, that wouldn't be fair to my client."

Quickly calculating what Bob paid six years ago for their yacht which had ten years on it when he bought it, she reckoned that a new seventy-six foot fully fitted out would bring a princely sum. That type of skill and business success in a man would be worthy of boasting; but he didn't.

"Do you have more orders?"

"Yes."

"I guess you can't rush something like that just to get to the next buyer."

"Not, really."

"Where's your yard? I'd like to stop by and see your work in progress."

Did she really just ask this man who must be twenty years her junior, to accept a self-invitation which he hadn't made?

"Sure. It's Blair's near the top of the creek. Don't come next week, I'm taking my boys fishing before school starts. We'll be back on Thursday. And come about four. We don't work on Sunday. A Saturday would be better."

"But school starts this Tuesday."

"They're sophomores in college."

"You must be kidding. You can't be old enough to have college age sons. They're both sophomores? How can that be?"

"Well Evie, I'm forty-six and the boys are twins. One's at Purdue, the other boy's at NC State, both studying engineering."

"Will they build boats one day too?"

"No, I started with my father when I was ten. You need to have the knack for it and desire. He knew I had it and so did I. Mark has it but doesn't want to build boats. Gray doesn't have it at all and is glad about it. I'm afraid it will end with me. They're both into aeronautics."

I'm an idiot she thought. Why can't I at least think before I ask something so embarrassingly dumb?

"What a stupid question, I have twin grandsons. You look much younger."

"Look at you. How can you be a grandmother? Isn't there a state law about marrying so young?"

Now his turn at mild stupidity.

"Do you think it has anything to do with living on the Bay?" Evie asked.

"I think it has everything to do with it if people take care of themselves."

"Have you met anyone interesting tonight?"

"You mean the lady they tried to fix me up with? They told you? I couldn't think of anything clever to say to her. She thought the food, the wine, the house, the view, everything was 'delicious.' I think it's her favorite word."

"What did you think of her?"

"I have to tell you, I thought she was 'delicious' and very nice."

Evie laughed broadly at Frankie's honesty and humor.

"I have a divorce."

He said that as if 'I have a stigma or I have a disease' that he wished he didn't have and damn it, she thought that she sounded as if she cared if he had met anyone interesting, which it did.

"Yes, I did know about that. Does your ex-wife live down here?"

"No, she lives in Westchester, in New York. She's a waitress at a hotel up there. She left here when the boys were six, got mixed with some bad people, fell into drugs and just left one day with this fellow and another couple. I tried hard but couldn't help her. We didn't hear from her for four years. The boys go to visit her a couple times a year. They say she's real healthy now, a little overweight but healthy. They still love her. She's their mother."

Driving home that night she pleased herself by recounting their conversation. She might possibly visit the boat yard which had been in Solomons for decades. His work sounded interesting; and how long had she been playing that Buffet CD?

Only a week later Evie fussed and tried to pass that Saturday but the time idled and stalled all day. Had he mentioned Saturday after four to ask her out for an early light dinner afterwards? She dressed as if she hoped he would; maybe a little too dressy. In her heart she admitted that she could not wait to see and talk to him again. She arrived ten minutes early.

❖ ❖ ❖ ⛵ ❖ ❖ ❖

THE ROAD TO HAMPTON ROADS

The parade was heard to become the best ever. Never had such an array of well polished and original participants applied to the festival committee for entrance to the annual event. As the floats, bands and kids dressed like a spat marshaled together, the palatable excitement measured itself by the cloud of frosted breaths of the hundreds of marchers. If ever a finer early November Saturday could be remembered, no locals were trying. In the fifty-two year history, visitors were expected to set a new record. The leaves of golden and reddened hues found themselves mostly underfoot but enough of them remained attached aloft as a reminder of their recent glory. In a losing battle with the next rainy windswept morning, they still provided a colorful canopy and hint to the season. The weather for the day promised.

Davis and his buddies had been in Urbanna since Thursday evening. They had made this annual pilgrimage since their parents started bringing them there as children. The firemen's parade on

Friday evening had been their favorite event as youngsters. Meeting their friends from school and sampling the fresh oysters and other fine delicacies of delicious seafood evolved later as parental restraints lessened. Now on their own, they marked their calendars early in the year for the festival nine months hence and only two months removed from the last event.

The young men came to join a former fraternity brother who taught at a county high school and who had become a father recently. At twenty-eight, all but the teacher had gone to work in Davis's father's brokerage firm in Richmond and made more in a few months than the teacher earned in a year. Successful, young and eminently eligible bachelors, they enjoyed social events at home but preferred the broader realm of regional gatherings all year long and the Oyster Festival was 'the pearl' according to Davis. When standing side by side one could know about them and the cloth from which they all had been cut; fine, strong and expensive. Almost identical in height and build, anyone could have guessed that their relaxed attitude and common geniality had come to them through no accident. If Davis, the sole heir of a prominent Richmond family, would meet a young woman who intrigued him at the festival or anywhere, that someone would be beautiful, bright, witty, charming and intelligent. At six-feet two, his average good looks, warm smile with perfect teeth and rather shy manner presented him as a magnet to any interested fair maiden and most were interested and most were not maidens. He had morphed into that certain guy that women rather love and men rather like. To his credit, the obvious conceit that could have been his bore no resemblance to his unaffected personality. On a bad day he could be a bit short and uppity with people but never with friends or family. They all belonged to that certain circle that thrived among this modern gentry. With tacit consent and understanding they knew who belonged and who didn't. For his part Davis had never tried to pick up a woman in his life. He appeared upon a scene and chose among those who chose him. If no one chose him, he did without.

Waiting for the oyster shucking contest to begin, they sat together at a popular bistro on the town's dock that Captain John Smith may have sailed or rowed past, maybe even alit just over four hundred years ago. Crowded with an already overflow of early patrons, the swelling day trippers began to add atmosphere and frivolity to the host of events which over the decades had hastened their popularity and added to the town's appeal and charm. Many first time festival visitors vowed to and indeed did return in different seasons, such was the attraction of this beautiful setting on the Rappahannock just up from the Bay.

"Davis, don't you want to have a serious relationship, be in love, get married and have a family like our 'professor' here?"

"Oh, absolutely Rob, I think the 'prof' is the happiest of all four of us. He's always known that he wanted to teach. He and Amanda love each other only and they have a great little kid. He's working on his master's at night and they enjoy the simple things in life. We could do worse than follow his good example. Don't you think Mickey?"

After the slightest pause, the four, even the 'professor', burst into hilarity but not laughing so heartily that any imported beer was spilled, sprayed or spit out.

"Sure, we'll trade our life styles to settle down when were older, maybe in our thirties. My father was forty when he married. Why should we take one little striped bass when the

Bay is full of nicer ones. No offense, Professor, I'm happy that you're happy. It's just that Davis, Eddie and I don't get it, at least not yet."

"No offense taken Mickey, I'm not saying being married at times is easy, and somehow the tiffs and disagreements Amanda and I have are just as intense and probably as many as when we were dating and engaged. When you live with someone though, are married to them, the little to-dos go away quicker and you learn how to avoid them in the first place. Having a kid helps too. No matter what, we know how he depends on us both. Even when we're not exactly 'crazy' in love with each other at certain times, our common love for him keeps love in the atmosphere. We soon realize how petty other things are compared to the three of us being together. What about you Eddie? You and Jennifer have been kind of together for over two years now. What's up?"

"It's off for now. She and her parents wanted me to have a 'pre-nup.' She really got offended when I said 'no.' I haven't talked to her this week. It's her girl friends and parents who are telling her to do this and don't do that. I'm not dating them. I'm dating her."

"Wait, Jennifer doesn't have any money. You don't have any money. Besides that old skiff and your golf clubs, what else do you own? I don't get it."

"Well Rob, my sister and I have that house in Virginia Beach but it's not that. Virginia is a fifty-fifty divorce state. She wants a guarantee of certain amount if we split up before five years and about half that amount if we divorce between five and ten years and more if there are any children. After that she figures I'll be worth enough to take her chances."

Davis, repelled at this notion, couldn't believe this absurdity.

"Are you saying that she wants your parents to guarantee this money? That's just a lot of bull. I thought 'pre-nups' were asked for by the one with the gold, not the other way 'round. What do your mom and dad think of this?"

"Are you kidding, Davis? I would never tell them and I know you guys will keep this to yourselves and your other twenty best friends. My folks aren't that fond of her lately anyway. If this got back to them, it would be all over. Besides I'm starting to see that bartender over in the city and I feel good about that 'cause I know that's not going anywhere."

"O.K. let me get this straight. Eddie, you're cheating on your girlfriend and unofficial fiancée who wants your family to promise her a lump sum buyout if the marriage doesn't work out; assuming the break-up is gong to be your fault, which it will. Davis, you and Mickey are just dogs in heat and pretty much leading a pointless, debauched existence with nothing to look forward to except the your next conquest whether it's a debutant, co-ed or a bar fly. No, no, I'll take my life any day. Besides, I get to have a debased lifestyle vicariously through your pathetic lives. Do you really feel good about yourselves and the day ahead when you wake up in the morning? Are you really happy with the path to nowhere you both seem to be on?"

"Yeah, isn't it great? Davis and I wouldn't know how good we have it if we didn't have you jokers to compare it to, right my brother?"

"My 'existence' may seem meaningless but what's the sense of having a goal if I don't know what it is? I've got a good job, a townhouse two blocks from the James and you bums to hang around with. My parents babysit my dog when I go out of town. Life is good."

With the philosophy of life solved over a single beer each, they found themselves engrossed at the oyster shucking contest. Deep love and appreciation abounded for the Bay by all those living so close to its watershed, just up its rivers and on the Bay itself. For all their shallowness, they at least got this. All the inhabitants drew on the Bay's pleasures every day of the year without thinking. The wonder of its harvest of gifts amazed and blessed them all in some manner. For the locals and those who had come and made themselves natives, young and old from the Susquehanna to the James, from the Chester to the Pocomoke, on both sides of the Bridge and Tunnel, this was a beautiful part of the world in which to live and hopefully work. They didn't find the need to verbalize the wonders and benefits of Chesapeake Bay living to each other or especially to strangers who wouldn't understand anyway. Words aren't that useful, powerful or descriptive compared to life's experience. So sometimes with raucous cheering for the adept skill of the shuckers, the men knew this special day embodied all the good of the Bay and were made happy by it.

The young teacher and his peers brought their students on the Thursday of festival week for demonstrations and educational exhibits conducted by The Chesapeake Bay Foundation, Living Shorelines and other conservators of the Bay's ecology and heritage. Middlesex County, like almost every municipality which abutted the Bay, possessed a rich history worthy of its preservation. The 'prof,' a chemistry teacher, relished the forum which allowed him to instruct and inspire students about the science, threats and protection of all its waters. He felt if this meaningful education had begun only a couple of generations ago, the Bay and its rivers would have fewer problems and be easier to solve but better late than never.

The young woman decided to finally ask Davis to move from one side to the other or to stand still altogether. She wasn't short but still how could she see over or around him as he craned his neck while watching the parade? His agile movements made them unable for her to predict. If she moved up or down a few yards along the route, his lean body seemed to follow her from the front. He couldn't have done better if he were facing her.

"Excuse me, I can hardly see because you keep bobbing and weaving in front of me."

"I'm very sorry ma'am, I apologize."

Without turning to face his accuser, he sidled up to a just vacant spot and she knew that he attempted to remain somewhat still. She had heard that accent only a few times before but knew its origin and a little about the region and those who spoke with it.

When he did espy her, then next to him, that certain unexplainable yet undeniable sense of attraction overtook the visually smitten young man. The woman's beauty showed none of the signs which would mistake her for glamorous. Yet with only the slightest imagination one easily could picture her winner of any beauty contest, including the one against the true beauties vying for the local crown as they passed by on the inventive floats in this year's parade. Maybe the smile, as illuminating as his own, drew his attention. Dressed in a pair 'New Balance' cross training shoes, a black ribbed sweater, jeans and a light weight forest green nylon jacket, she wore a just purchased *Crabbiest Cookbook* baseball hat through which she had pulled her medium length auburn hair through the back and tied in a pony tail with two simple rubber bands. He could hardly guess that it was she whose view he had obstructed. The well disciplined, strong yet courteous intonation and timber surprised him when she eventually volunteered to being the polite hectorer who had asked him 'to stand still.'

"You must be looking for someone in the parade for all the fidgeting."

He didn't quite get it yet.

"Well, yes I am. My cousin's kids are dressed up like a spat." At first she thought he said 'pats' which necessitated her to more dialogue.

"Did you say 'pat'? What are they?"

"No, spat, 's. p. a. t.,' they're baby oysters."

Spelling the word for her kept her just interested and he was becoming glad about it.

"Yes, I've seen all those children with oyster costumes. I liked the ones with the big hats. I saw one made out of paper Mache. The little girl had a sign in the open jaws of the oyster that said, 'I'm just a shell of my former self.' You're a local, right?"

"You bet. Well, I live about this side of Richmond. My name's Davis, may I know yours?"

"Kimberly, or Kim will do, that's what a lot of my friends call me."

"Fidgeting? Were you the lady who asked me to stop blocking her view? Somehow I thought she was an older, let me say, more mature woman. You're not as old as I am. Is this your first festival? I can't quite place your accent. It seems you may not have one."

"It's my first 'oyster' festival and thanks for the compliment. No, you couldn't guess where I'm from. It wouldn't be fair. I've moved and travelled quite a bit but I have resided in Virginia for the last year or so."

"Where about? I know Virginia fairly well."

"Oh, here and there, I spent some time in Arlington, some in Stafford County and now I'm living in the Hampton Roads area, but I'm not sure for how long."

"Say, you do get around. I live about ten miles from where I was born and five miles where I grew up. I guess I was thinking more down this way but I do know the Norfolk and Virginia Beach area."

"I've heard nice things about Virginia Beach. They say it's a great resort city and beach. I hope to be able to get down there later today."

"Well, this is probably not the best time of year for a getting a tan."

"The thing is my job may not keep me in the area that long. I've seen different parts of the country and it gives me an idea of where I might want to settle down afterwards. My two friends are around here somewhere, probably down checking out the contestants in the beauty contest. I had better give them a ring so we don't get too separated."

"Are your friends men?"

How could he have asked such an in inane and potentially suggestive question? If she were too offended he'd plow ahead if she'd allow him.

"Yes they are."

"I think my buddies are probably standing right next to them. Would you care to join me and sample some local fare, maybe get a beer?"

"I'd like that, but it's a little too early in the day for me and beer. Would any of the food go good with a diet Pepsi?"

"Well now, I'm glad you said Pepsi. I'm a stock holder."

This attempt at humor did not go over that well and he reminded himself to avoid any more self rewarding references along with the thoughtless queries. After her call, the new acquaintances made their way through the stalls and vendors. Kim sampled every dish recommended by Davis and to her mild surprise she savored each one with relish, liking each one in turn better than the others.

"O.K., so what was your favorite?"

"That's too hard to say. The stew is delicious. I never thought a soup made with these oysters could taste so incredible. I think the raw ones will take some time to acquire a taste for but I already think I could become a big fan. Is it true what they say about eating live oysters?"

"You mean the aphrodisiac, sex drive part? Personally I think it's true."

"Yes, I read about that too online but that's not what I meant. Are the oysters really alive when you eat them raw? It's nice to know you think they aid men in other areas but you seem healthy enough to be able to get along without too much help."

Another stupid thing to say and he's going to sound like Mickey and Eddie. He liked her and knew he was trying too hard, something he had little experience with and had no skill at.

"Yes, they are. I don't know of many foods eaten alive." He refused to elaborate in the dread of making another faux pas.

"That's why I liked the fried and baked ones. What are those called with the spinach? I liked them best of all."

"Oysters Rockefeller. Do you know why? It's said because they're green like money, or because they're so rich. After they were created and became popular, John D. Rockefeller was the richest man in the country. Actually the original Rockefellers weren't made with spinach at all. My mother claims her family lent some money and tobacco to the original chef's family in New Orleans in exchange for the original recipe during The Spanish American War in 1899. She makes them to this day supposedly following the original, passed down verbally through the years. My father thinks this is just hearsay and nobody but 'Antoine's' in New Orleans knows the original recipe. He says that kind of lore is one of those word of mouth fables that survive, especially in the South over generations from those times. He thinks it's like whispering a funny story around a cocktail party. By the time the third person whispers the joke to the fourth, little remains of the original story begun only minutes before."

"I'll take your word for it. Do people still have cocktail parties? I rather wish they did. I like the idea of the men in suits and ties and the women in 'cocktail' dresses. Everyone stands around a piano and fireplace sipping martinis, chatting wittily about current events, the latest movies and best sellers. So what's the secret recipe? Will you have to kill me if you give it up?"

"No, I don't think that it's classified 'top secret' anymore. Mother will give it to anyone who asks if you applaud her dish. She says to remember 'CATS BOOTY.' That stands for Capers, Anisette, Tabasco, Spinach – Butter, Olive (oil), Onions, Tablespoon (of parsley), Yellow (lemons for garnish). That's not to mention bread crumbs made fresh from a French baguette, fennel, garlic, celery leaves and parmesan cheese; and don't forget the oysters. Altogether there can be about eighteen ingredients."

"That's a lot to remember. Eighteen ingredients, don't you think that's over egging the pudding? How about I buy a cookbook? I saw several in one of the little stores here. I like to cook but don't have a chance that often lately."

"Try *The Oyster Cookbook* by Whitey Schmidt. He lives and writes on the Bay. How come you don't get to cook too often, nobody to cook for? What do you do for a living?"

"I'm a Marine, USMC."

"You're not! I mean the Marines; you just don't look like a Marine."

"Is it because I'm a woman? That's O.K., I hear that sometimes. If I had my 'Dress Blues' on you might get a better picture."

"I mean I think that's great. I want to say, thank you for serving. Are you a specialist of some kind?"

She thought the sentiment well meant, his sincerity genuine born from good manners.

"Each one of us is a 'specialist.' I'm an interpreter and language officer among other things but for now that's my job."

Entranced by her open and lively personality, a certain charm and prettiness, he wanted to ask her for a date or something but knew he felt strangely awkward. His past experiences mostly involved having the women make the overture. This was different. Davis discovered a little determination attached to his psyche. No amount of reservation about Kim's work would prevent him from pursuing her good opinion of him.

"So where are you stationed now? Is that why you're in Virginia?"

"Well, I'm on shore leave for two weeks. I'll be stationed in the Hampton Roads area."

"What then, where do you think you'll go?"

"I must tell you that we aren't to discuss deployments except with close family members. I'm sure you understand. From one December I'll be in Norfolk. We're going to look at houses to rent in Virginia Beach for a couple of weeks starting tomorrow. Did you know that Urbanna means 'City of Anne' in Latin? True to early seventeenth century custom, if a town wasn't named after an English city like Boston, Richmond or 'New' York, or after royalty Queen Annes, Jamestown etc., the governors in London dubbed a town often in Latin."

She didn't own any PepsiCo equities but she did have 'stock' and trade and Latin was one of her investments.

"I rather did know that. Must have been one the few days I was paying attention in school and I absolutely understand about too many questions. I'm happy to have blocked your view otherwise we might not have met."

"Oh, I don't know. I would have thought of something." He smiled.

Davis invited her and her friends, two young able bodied lieutenants like Kim, to a small midday brunch near Urbanna the next morning. Rob and Eddie were also there and were duly impressed with Kim. Her friends exemplified what he thought a Marine should look like and promised himself to get to the gym he'd joined three months ago yet had visited only once. Kim and her friends enjoyed the day. The guys got along well. Davis, Eddie and Rob had never served in the military but enough common ground among the five guys existed. Whether by design, on purpose or carefulness on all their parts, the conversation never neared the topic of politics, foreign policy or war except that a new president had been elected that week and all were hoping for a better future for America. Davis noted that the two recently commissioned men paid no particular deference to Kim and the ease and conviviality increased as the small party continued into the early afternoon. Before they drove away, he asked if he could call and see her again. She handed him her card on which she had written her cell number on the back.

By the time she reached her senior year in high school, Kim knew that her small town in the midwest held few viable options for her. Reluctantly she attended the junior college in the next town, became drawn into the language department because of innate abilities and an undeniable desire which drove her to take all courses in the syllabus, French, German and Spanish. In high school, three years of French and Latin more than prepared her for the college courses, I & II and she devoted her time conquering the other two. She had wondered if she weren't so talented would she still be fascinated by foreign tongues and guessed she would be. It came to her that the fascination was not only the vocabulary, syntax and grammar of the languages but the idea that they were spoken in far away lands by different peoples with histories and customs alien from her own. This excited her. The place she called home had begun to enclose her spiritually. A place she loved and home to the people she adored instigated a passion within her to leave to literally see the world, to discover if there were other places as nice as hers. She may return one day after her travels if only because of the mid western goodness of its people. She had heard of 'Southern Hospitality' and knew now it to be true but without any self prevarication, no group of people in the country was kinder and more generous than her neighbors from the broad plains and curling rivers of her childhood.

A grandfather who had served in the Marine Corps from

'66 to '72 became her inspiration from an early age. As a child, she loved to visit him. He related many stories about the parts of the world and people he had seen without telling her that Uncle Sam served as his travel agent. Not until junior high school did she learn of his embassy duty in Europe and the tours which he had served in Vietnam; and only then because her mother revealed that her father had served. He had never told her any horrid details, not even that he had fought in a terrible war. As she grew older, the little girl developed into a big girl and with that natural progression, her interest and curiosity followed along with her maturity in all things including more specific queries to this seemingly uncomplicated and stoic man. As a nineteen year old, he had been drafted into the Army but chose The Marines instead because his best friend had joined up right after high school and wrote to encourage him to follow. As details of her grandfather's career revealed itself to her, she grew more amazed at his humility and tempered pride which were only a few of the ingredients of the good man. She knew she loved him with all her heart but when her mother showed her two Purple Hearts and a Bronze Star with the accommodation describing the details of the actions which he had taken with valor and bravery to more than justify this honor, she felt more esteemed adoration and admiration for him than she thought possible. He had risked his life to save others, twice. Somewhere in the back of her mind a subconscious thought planted itself. For then, all she hoped for sprung from the promise she had made to herself after she obtained her two year associate's degree.

She enlisted soon after spending a week on vacation in Fort Lauderdale. A track team and lacrosse standout in school prepared her well for boot camp at Parris Island. Still she hardened herself mentally and physically for what she knew would be a most demanding regimen. After all the requisite tests, the Corps and the Navy found themselves to have a natural born linguist on their hands. She promptly found herself stationed to the Defense Language Institute in Monterrey, California. After twenty-six months of total immersion studies she confounded her professors and elders with rapid progress. These were not the European languages of her school days but Arabic, Farsi, Urdu and Pashto, spoken in; Iraq, Iran, Pakistan and Afghanistan. All marines are trained as riflemen. She honed this skill as often as possible, received her commission and transferred to Henderson Hall in the shadow of The Pentagon. From there her orders took her to Quantico, then Chesapeake, Virginia, there to attend the basic security guard force and after this brief respite of ten days to up the road to Norfolk. Without much guessing she knew she had made her last sojourn in the States for quite a while. In fact her orders awaited her. As a member of 'FAST,' 'Fleet Antiterrorism Security Team,' her days in the land of pleasant living were numbered.

When Davis called two days later she agreed to meet him in Virginia Beach where she and her friends had rented Rob's house for a very low, nominal price. While her friends went their own way, the stock broker and Marine went to dinner where he introduced her to more exotic oyster dishes. After starting out with a dozen of the saltier raw 'seasides' from Chincoteague, they sampled 'Bingo' and fried oyster fritters. He left for home early but asked if they could meet the next evening. She volunteered to drive up to Richmond. That night they chatted with sincerity about more intimate issues, hopes and plans. Kim held no definite idea for herself save for the one possibility of making a career with her current employer. Beyond the date of her next re-enlistment, she knew of no other ambition. Nothing excited her. Explaining that she had become too occupied with her current work, she prodded Davis to reveal his picture of the future.

"I'll settle down one day, get married I guess. I'd like to have a family. Yeah, I'm really thinking a lot lately about being married with a couple of kids. I don't want to have an only child. I'm one and sometimes I wish I had a brother."

"Only a brother, didn't you want a couple of sisters?"

"I have mother. She's been kind of the female companion in my life. As I got older she became my friend and confidant. Don't get me wrong after college she wanted me to get a place of my own, didn't want me moving back in the house. She said it was time to cut the cord."

"Do you see them very often?"

"I work for my father but I see mother more. He's either out playing golf with clients, in New York or attending some luncheon. We have meetings at the office each Tuesday but he seems to miss every other one. No, my mother is my best friend apart from the guys. We dine together a couple of times a week and I play with her in the mixed doubles at the club, tennis and golf. She's always been my biggest supporter and fan."

"Sounds like she'd be hard to replace."

"I don't want to replace her. I just know how thrilled she'll be when I find the right girl. Personally, I think she'll treat her like the daughter she never had. If I ever gave her grandchildren I'm afraid she'd forget who I am. If you ever met her you'd understand. She'd like you and you her."

A pregnant pause halted this oedipal salutation to his mother. Kim had never known her father who left her mother shortly after marrying her six months before she was born. Though she carried his last name, it was her mother's father who provided Kim all the genuine male attributes so sought after by girls in their fathers. He may not have been her natural father but no child could have asked for a better father and parent.

"Tell me about yourself and your family. I seem to be doing all the talking."

"I had a normal childhood. I grew up in a small town in Iowa and really lived the all American life you see on television. I played sports, worked at a pharmacy and dated the captain of the football team. After I went to a community college I kind of wanted to find some work which would allow me to travel. I guess I found that job alright."

"You amaze me. I've never known anyone as open and honest as you. Were you always like that or did the Marines instill that in you?"

"The Marines reinforced whatever it is. My grandfather set the good example for me. He taught me by doing and not talking and became the guiding force in my life."

"Is he an ex-Marine?"

"There's no such thing as an 'ex-Marine' only a former Marine and yes, he is and yes, that's why I joined."

The next day he took her out in his father's cabin cruiser to the Bay only a few miles from the marina. The early morning hour opened brightly as the large twin engine boat cut the through the light, choppy water of the middle Bay toward the sun rise.

Kim stared aft at times as the powerful craft left her cone shaped wake behind in a prism of glint, glare and glimmer. The day was brisk and cool but not especially rough. Other than the rivers of Missouri, Nebraska and Illinois which included the

Mississippi well north of St. Louis, she had never been on a large body of water except in amphibious training. The excursion exhilarated her. Davis brought the powerful craft about, headed back west and up the Rappahannock River to Irvington. They lunched on two dozen clams, half steamed in water, the other half in white wine and fresh mussels in the same type of wine, lemon and garlic butter sauce. To wash down this midday feast, Davis ordered a bottle Virginia Viogner and the light crispness of the wine seemed to drink like water. They decided against another bottle but both were sorely tempted. The thrill of the morning intoxicated them more than the wine ever could.

Strong palatable feelings of affection, desire and passion visited them each. No amount of denying the raw yet warm attraction served a purpose for very long and they knew instinctively that the other had never been so ardently affected. By the time the cruiser reached the channel of the creek to tie back up, neither had wanted the journey to end. They each were in fear that tying up at the slip to end the cruise would be a metaphor for the end of this love which had just begun. Their concern lacked any real truth and such an idea that this ardor would or could wane soon struck them as notional. They stayed in each others arms all night; their love making kept to the rolling rhythm of the moored boat. At times she moved gently not straining, easy in her berth. As night morphed into the early hours the pulsating high tide washed through the marina with energy and distinctive force. Then calm, soft, almost tender movements rendered her at ease again, relaxed in the safety of her surroundings.

The pair stayed inseparable through the following weekend, an anniversary of the festival. Kim, practical in all matters, phoned her friends daily to let them know her whereabouts and the happy disposition in which she found herself. They offered to refund her third of the rent but naturally she declined as they would have had the situation been reversed. The three were genuinely fond of each other and the two men regarded her as a Marine and their equal. As beautiful as she was, she had experienced only one salacious trespass from an ill adjusted platoon member in boot camp. After four weeks this misfit found himself a civilian again not only because of Kim but because of his weird anti-social behavior overall. His words, actions and reason for discharge were surely noted in some federal data base. The men and women received intense behavioral education in the rules, laws and accepted behavior of Marines, officers and enlisted. Theirs shone as a microcosm of society at large. Everything that occurs in life may exhibit itself on a smaller scale in the Corps and it does. Civilians in general though, should be so well behaved. The difference is the common sense training and distinct purpose; to achieve their objectives and protect and guard one another. Society is rather untrained thus and is the worse for it. Both genders exhibit respect for their comrades. It would be just as heinous if a woman Marine behaved offensively. Just as in life though, things can and do happen.

After fetching the rest of her civilian clothes and gear she stayed with him in what he called a townhouse. While the home attached itself to another making it a duplex instead, her perplexed awe confounded any understanding of how someone as young as Davis could own such a beautiful house set in an Eden like park of like mini-mansions.

When queried he only responded, "I had hoped that you'd like it. I love living here."

"I've never seen or heard of an attached home with four floors, two verandas, patios everywhere and three garages. You must be rich."

"No, I'm not. Dad and mother are though. Well mother's the one who brought the money to the marriage. Dad came from a very good family with all the right connections like southern aristocracy but they were broke. He had that charm and manners though, handsome too according to mother. He's still a great looking guy. It's been said she and a few other wealthy debutantes bid on him and mother won. They put half down on this place so I could afford the mortgage. I'll pay them back though when I sell it, if they'll take it. We bought at the right time, six years ago when I got out of school. These places have gone through the roof since then. There's been a slow down in real estate this year but my neighborhood has held its own. Dad is real smart about money. He went to work for my grandfather, mother's dad, mostly managing the family's investments. Then he started caring for friends of mother and the business just blossomed."

"What were the family investments?"

"Tobacco, peanuts and whatever else the land gave them. They owned quite a bit at one time. Dad sold some of it off, developed some and kept the rest. He's always telling mother, 'We don't want cash crops we want cash making cash.'"

"What do you do for your dad, if you don't mind?"

"Eddie and I started a fund within dad's company which mostly invests in the banking industry. Dad gave us an excellent client base, twisted a few arms and we were off. We've been flying pretty high until just recently but I'm sure it's just an aberration. Everything will go right back up after the inauguration. So, are

45

you anxious to meet mother tonight? She's just dyin' to meet you. You'll like the hotel where we're dining tonight. They would take me there if I won a golf match or for my birthday. That mother chose the hotel restaurant means meeting you is something special. You know how much I love you and she will too. You are all I can talk about when we call each other."

"I love you, Davis. I'd love you if you were one of those watermen we spoke with at the docks the other morning. I respect what you do, yet those are the type of working men whom I grew up around. You do know how difficult it will be when we're apart. I've told you my tour will last months and months."

"That sounds like an eternity to me but this feeling I have for you will give me all resolve and strength I need. In fact, it grows more every day. I'm plain worried about you. Please promise me, promise us that you won't let anything happen. I couldn't take it."

"Nothing is going to happen to me. I am as well trained as those who'll be around me. We know, have to know, if we do our jobs right, we'll all be back. I love the Chesapeake and intend to spend the rest of my life near it."

Whether they were early or his mother late, Kim couldn't tell since Davis hadn't told her the time of the meeting. Always striving to be prompt, she was glad they arrived first. After thirty minutes Davis' mother rather burst upon them in a sight huff.

Only glancing at Kim with a slight smile she stood directly in front of and close to Davis and recounted to her son the perplexed afternoon she had endured and for a full minute looked or rather gazed only at him. Then with the zeal of a convert, the woman made her most profuse regrets to Kim for her tardiness. Not exactly knowing how to respond to this dramatic apologia, Kim smiled and nodded a pleasant acquiescence as if she understood, which she didn't. If some meeting of the charity committee at the club ran frightfully past its allotted time frame because some new ad hoc members were unfamiliar with the adopted by-laws, she just couldn't be so rude as to call them out of order. To end the meeting in order to rush out to meet her son and the new woman in his life, even though his mother was the chairwoman, really went against the spirit of charity itself. So, she was horribly sorry.

For cocktails they sat in front of the fireplace in the antebellum hotel bar. Davis revealed to Kim before she arrived that his mother, Mrs. Eudora Lee Desmond, nee James, Dora Lee to her friends and family, possessed certain quirks which may seem to make her a rather odd bird at first. He vouchsafed for her goodness and generosity in admirable terms which did alleviate some genuine concern Kim felt. Mrs. Desmond seemed taller than Kim but that could have been owed to the different height of their heeled shoes. Kim guessed she must be in her mid-fifties but appeared much younger, until she spoke. Perhaps the charming accent and manners seemed to date her to earlier and more genteel generations. The similarities between Kim and his mother were unmistakable though. Both women shared the same coloring, blue-green eyes and a certain confidence in their own beauty. Kim knew, as did Dora Lee, in that unspoken feminine instinct, that the resemblance existed without contradiction. The older adult's figure couldn't have altered much since her young womanhood and she wore her expensive suit as well as was possible. Although she lighted a cigarette from a gold lame mesh case with ease and alacrity, the fact that she smoked at all also hinted at betrayal of an age not consistent with her youthful appearance. When the white jacketed server came to take their cocktail order, Mrs. Desmond ordered a pitcher of very dry expensive gin martinis with all garnishes on the side, it told Kim that this woman had good tastes and that she took charge without waiting for any slightly embarrassing indecisions. No fan of gin martinis, Kim sipped hers out of politeness.

"Darlin', you're just too beautiful to be a soldier. I hope you don't mind if I smoke. It's a way of life here."

Without waiting for Kim's reply, Davis burst in, "Marine, mother, Kim is in the Marines."

"Oh, I apologize, but I'm sure I wouldn't know the difference. I had a second cousin once removed who was at VMI and became a pilot in the Marines. I never knew what happened to him. Davis what's all this rumblin' going on about the market? Your father has been in a tizzy these last couple of weeks. Have you and Edward made some horrible miscalculations about bank stocks?"

"I don't think so mother. I haven't paid much attention to it lately. I've been too busy falling in love with Kim. Besides I haven't heard anything from dad or Eddie on it."

"Oh well, you boys know what you're doin'. Kim, I am just the woman of the house who doesn't understand all these complicated tradin' practices. It was simpler in my daddy's day. We grew and sold crops from the fine land we owned in North Carolina and Virginia and put the money in the bank to save. He also bought crabs and oysters from the watermen and processed them to sell up the line. Alas, that business has gone to hell. Now, good heavens, you have to be a scientist to understand all the various types of investments. What do your Marines have planned for you? At least you won't have to go fight in any war. Davis said you'll be in Norfolk."

"Yes I will but I don't feel like it will be for long. I'm part of a battalion which secures the safety of naval installations and ships among other things against terrorism."

"Does that mean they'll send you over to the Middle East or some terrible place like that?"

"Well, that's where our services are needed the most these days."

"Kim's a translator, mother. She speaks I don't know how many languages."

"Actually I'm an interpreter but I still share in many of the duties my battalion has been assigned to."

"Good lord, do mean to tell me that you have the same job description as a man and that you'll be in harm's way, that you'll have a gun?"

"We're Marines first and yes, we all carry our own weapons."

"Kim has assured me that she'll be safe. She's very well trained. We both have a lot to live for."

After dinner, at which Dora Lee chose all the courses and wine, she drank five cups of coffee probably since she had drunk the most wine and martinis and knew that Davis would not let her drive or make her take a cab had she not. She then invited Kim and Davis to a dinner party at a friend's home that Saturday night. This social gathering would have extended an invitation to Davis except that it was couples only and none his 'dates' in recent memory were suitable. The fact that they were asked, meant that his mother's high standard for an acceptable woman in his life had been met by Kim. Not so sure she should have to meet anyone's good opinion other than his, Kim treaded lightly with the only man she had ever loved. Kim needed a new dress for the occasion and found one in a Richmond department store.

The host's home sat on knoll with sweeping vistas down the James River and everyone could not have been more pleasant. No awkward questions about her job or employer punctuated the conversations but she knew that most everyone knew. She met Mr. Desmond and liked him immediately. Davis' broad toothy smile, thick hair and easy manner were only a few of the many characteristics which definitely made Davis his son. In a small group in the library including his father, one of the men warned her to be careful of Mr. D.

"He's a notorious bottom pincher, honey."

The entire evening Davis devoted most of his attention to her. He made introductions to each member of the gathering and appeared quietly protective in the way that helped her feel at ease and be herself. Maybe the few misgivings she'd had about this whirlwind romance were only instinctive safeguards. After all, he would remain here and wait for her.

The following Sunday she left him for the first time since their third date. He had to get back to work and she would return to the house in Virginia Beach to spend a day or two with her friends. Kim called the two men on Saturday to alert them of her return in two days so they would not be caught unawares in some situation with female company which would be more embarrassing to them than to her.

Kim would report for duty on the coming Friday and already a tightening in her heart began press on the true love and emotions she felt for Davis. He had mentioned engagement and she considered it with close attention but in the end both thought it could wait until she returned. At first she thought how difficult it might be while she served thousands of miles from home but thought otherwise. Their love would sustain her. Instead of desperately longing for him, a brighter, more optimistic attitude overcame her. She would welcome her work with even more enthusiasm knowing that each day that passed would bring them back together. Thousands of families and loved ones are separated because of their service; she would not be alone.

While Davis worked, she cleaned his house, washed clothes and shopped for household items either sorely needing replacing or lacking altogether. He was met in the evenings with a beautifully prepared dinner not of shell fish or seafood but broiled lamb chops with Brussels' sprouts and potatoes au gratin, or a filet mignon. One evening Davis broiled crab cakes from another old family recipe and she thought it the tastiest dish she had ever tried. Their meetings would be curtailed after she reported. Even if they could only be together for a few hours after work, he would make the short journey to the Hampton area, stay in Rob's house or a motel then drive up to the work the next day.

That Friday came soon enough and she left him at four-thirty in the morning after loving and caressing each other since dinner. No tears, no regrets, only smiles that said no amount of separation could interfere with their love, except to make it stronger. The love making and no sleep left them both exhilarated and energized by the loving promise of the future.

That night they spoke by phone several times since she had to interrupt conversations for short periods that he assumed involved her work. They made plans for the few hours she'd be allowed off base on Saturday. When he failed to call by four that afternoon, she tried him and left a message. With no call by six she tried him again with the same result. She didn't allow her mind to wander to accident or mishap. He would call soon. At nine sharp she rang again. The phone answered. There must have been an accident.

"Why hello darlin' this is Dora Lee."

"I've been trying to reach Davis. We were supposed to meet this evening. Is he O.K.?"

"That depends on your definition of O.K. Physically he's fine but I fear he's a bit down in the dumps but he gets over these moods in a rather timely manner."

"Oh, I'm so happy he's alright. May I speak with him please?"

"Well, he's not here. He went out with his father to a football game in Charlottesville this morning. They always spend the night with friends. I am glad they do. When those boys go to one of those UVA games, I swear they have a better time than the students."

"Mrs. Desmond, this is not like Davis. He said he'd call and we'd be together this weekend. I've left him messages. Why did he leave his phone? Did he forget it? He'd know that I would try to call him. This doesn't make sense."

"Dear Kim, I really don't think you've known Davis quite long enough to determine what is like him or not like him. All I can tell you is that he's in Charlottesville with his father and friends. I am sure he'll get back to you at some point."

"Mrs. Desmond, Davis and I love each other very much. I'm about to be deployed half way around the world in a matter of days. We are to spend as many moments as possible together until then."

"Yes, well, his father and I had a little chat with him about that over here last night. We both realize he's kind of fond of you but do really think it wise to pursue this little shipboard like romance? Sorry for the pun, honey. Personally I just can't see it."

"I have every intention of pursuing a life with the man I love with or without your seeing or approving."

"Now listen child, ever since you got your military claws in him everything has changed for the worse. He and Edward made some egregious investments that lost more than half of their client's money and now they're clamoring for what's left in cash. This has put a terrible financial strain on my husband and me. As a result our marriage and happy home have suffered as well. Now, you show up and do whatever it is you do to and for my boy and he stops working and plays with you all day. He barely keeps me on the phone for a minute lately when we used to chat for an hour each day. You're a regular Jonah. I suggest you go wherever you must and leave him alone."

"Mrs. Desmond, I hadn't met Davis when he made those investments. Did you ask Davis to leave his phone with you on purpose so you could tell me all this?"

"No, Darlin', I didn't have to ask him. I've answered these calls for Davis before."

❖ ❖ ❖ ⚓ ❖ ❖ ❖

Annapolis Annie
(Or a Girl's Gotta Eat)

Somewhere in the history of man's eternal quest for woman there must be, written or unwritten, every conceivable ruse, scheme or plan put forth by him who must have that certain woman for his own as a life long mate; or at least for twenty-five minutes. In fact failing to woo, cajole and otherwise win this woman, an instinctive urge, well beyond his ability to control or understand this internal pounding of pent-up lust, will tell him simply to move on the next one. All the platitudes aside, 'Faint heart never won fair maiden', 'Dance the 'cosmic dance', the urge dominates. So it goes to the never ending quest for conjugal gratification, relief and release. Happy are most about this primal desire since this intangible animal magnetism, for better or worse, is how everyone got here. After the bitterness and ignominy of a failed partnership, which may or may not have produced progeny, the average, hapless male commences at the same starting point of the same path and probably to the same end as rendered him miserable in the first place. Without altering a thing, save for a new shirt from Kohl's, and in a pique of sheer folly, he presents himself on the open market of like souls, all usually aiming above his ability to attract a woman whose goal it is to attract someone beyond her reach. People like nice things. They prefer to surround themselves with objects that please their eye. Some are not so fussy and most settle, not too unhappily, for what they have and can afford to bear. The actual drive for carnal satisfaction is the true urge to propagate. Thankfully, offspring result in a most minute percentage of orgasmic meetings between the 'Opposite Sex.' Indeed, no one ever coined the phrase the 'Different Sex.' No, it has always been the former. Men shave their faces, women shave their legs. Men can go bald; women seem to have plenty of hair. The genitalia go in different directions. Yet if women and men could see an interactive, programmed model based and built on the psychological, temperamental and neurotic components of each gender, not only would they avoid the other in horror at the sight of this monstrous, unsightly manifestation, they may recoil, eschew and run from their own kind as well. Let there be little mistake that each pleasurable sexual union presents a shared closeness between partners at least for the moment, bar sex for sale, pretense to passion or simple indifference in bed. Apart from holding hands or a good morning kiss, in all healthy relationships each has their place and all carry whatever relative importance attached to them. So, the commonalities of desires of most inhabitants, based on generational positioning today, that is to say age, are guided and operate rather automatically. Or maybe more well put, would be the observation of a healthy freshman coed in her dorm room with like minded friends.

"Um, like, you know, I can't even imagine my grandparents doing it, like, not even when they were young, and like I don't even want to THINK about my own parents."

"OUuuuuuuuuuuuuuuuuuu!" being the general retort from all.

Eighteen year old boys have few discussions in this area so as to live up to and save their reputation for remaining callow, indolent and feckless. Ah, the generation upon which all coming generations depends. Has it always been thus? Yes, probably so.

Anne grew up in Anne Arundel County. Her grandparents pronounced the second part of the county, 'Aaron-dell.' She never knew why and never cared. A true beauty in high school, she dated boys in college when she was in the tenth grade. After dropping out after her junior year she led a semi-promiscuous yet safe existence through secretarial school. At nineteen she controlled three steady boy friends at once and had rings and other baubles to prove it. By twenty-one her stock as a legal secretary had risen at the large firm in Washington D.C. where the partners, associates and mail clerks had all taken their proverbial 'shot.' In the early eighties sexual revolutions had waned but the three martini lunch, corrupt business practices, glass ceilings and sexual harassment were doing a brisk business.

Leggy with a great butt, shapely hips, slim waist and other attributes that added to her pleasing personality, Anne liked her job and excelled at her work. After the first ten months on the job her Christmas bonus of a five hundred dollars exceeded that of other staffers with more tenure by double. While none of the support staff knew the exact amount of the partners' munificence, it became well rumored that it was twice the actual amount. By Easter the gossip mill had pegged the number at two to three thousand.

Completely oblivious to the contempt for her held by her co-workers, Anne commuted for two years from home before buying, with the co-signing aid of her immediate boss and his wife, an old but attractive well built town home on a tree lined street adjacent to St. John's College in Annapolis. She knew at once the house had more problems than character at the time but steeled herself against impending repair and restoration. Since she assumed a V.A. loan from the sellers, an approved appraiser dutifully didn't quite find the value to match the sales price because of the obvious flaws which would kill the deal.

After meeting with the appraiser at a rare second inspection, Anne found the man to be less strident in his opinions especially after their lunch in town. Soon after she reapplied a second coat of lipstick, the now obliging man gave her a list of sub-contractors for the necessary jobs and told her to be sure to use him as a reference. She had always been a good saver and now took on extra work on weekends at home for two fledgling attorneys in downtown Annapolis who had hung their shingle upstairs over a shoe store. Her next purchase bordered on near insanity for her as she paid for an expensive foreign coupe at one fifth the price of her house. Anne would brook no amount of scrimping when it came to items of necessity. In all other areas she happily settled for the least expensive. Whether born from insecurity or personality trait, she freely admitted to herself that she had become overly thrifty. The third and last personal must she demanded for herself was her wardrobe. Her clothes, purchased at the best department stores in the Washington area, became the talk of her expansive office, not only because of how stylishly well she wore them but for their obviously expensive, rich cut. Of course her haute couture only deepened the well of derision felt by her female co-workers. No amount of prurient slander was spared her and she knew of it but didn't care. After returning a garment to a top store for a ragged seam, the saleswoman made the return and refund so pleasant that Anne wondered to her aloud that the exchange came so easily. The woman informed Anne that some of the store's top clientele, rich women, bought, wore and returned items regularly. From that day Anne shaved seventy- percent of her wardrobe expense by returning three of every four purchases after she had worn them. In fact, she became so adept at this ploy that she could hide the garment's tags effortlessly with a wide belt or retagging the price tag with a tool purchased for that purpose. By keeping the clothes 'unmussed' as possible, she may get a wearing as many as twice. Since she paid good money for everything she bought, the stores were more than willing to accommodate her. Her fashionable appearance at the office only fueled the slander from the catty co-workers. Not wanting to press her luck, she returned the dresses, outfits and suits as soon as they had given her sufficient use but once she left a returnable hanging in the closet for almost a year. With trepidation Anne took the designer dress back with some chagrin but it was unwarranted since she was treated no differently as if she had purchased the item in the past week.

No true love had ever come to Anne so far. She remained content throughout her early twenties and dated more sporadically. Only the very best looking men held her regard and yet she always seemed to find some tragic flaw in them. Many were overly vain, self-congratulatory preening schmos. Some had watery, weak natures that belied their handsome faces and good builds. The rest simply owned humdrum, boring personalities which put them in the category of the average guy. More than a few were incorrigible inebriates who would fall asleep by eight 'o clock. Well aware of her appeal, it became amusing the amount of time, trouble and effort men would undertake to curry her favor. She wondered if it could only be her sex appeal and decided it must be. Free and open sex had been a staple as a teenager but she grew disaffected with all the panting of her passion-hungry partners. After all, she didn't cook. In fact she loved eating well but loathed cooking. She refused to keep house or wash clothes preferring to hire a professional maid who came once a week at a time when she could ill afford the expense. At home, she mostly ate frozen pouches of foods which could be prepared in boiling water. Mending, sewing and altering were as foreign to her as bridge building. Certainly aware that her car and home must be maintained, Anne took on the extra work to afford the care of her two large possessions. If however, the service manager at the dealership would barter some of the work for some flittering and his harmless glance at above-the-knee thigh as she slowly slid out from behind the wheel while he held her door open, she accepted; saving the few extra dollars pleased her.

By thirty, her home had been restored to her tasteful satisfaction. A private parking space in her office building made the now longer, time consuming commute more tolerable and her salary and vacation time had tripled in the less than ten years. She often traveled with the attorneys around the country for proceedings, conferences and depositions more as a general factotum than stenographer or secretary. All the reservations, communications, transportation and ancillary staffing needs relied entirely on her. She made favorable impressions on the out of town companies who hired her firm as well as opposing counsel. The intelligence, charm and appearance she brought to otherwise boring meetings gave kudos to her bosses for being so clever as to having her on their staff. Of all the major cities in which she attended to her bosses, she preferred ones on the water, Charleston, San Diego, San Francisco. After travelling, she realized another reason she had chosen Annapolis. It wasn't because of her family up the road, it was the water. Anne had never been close to her mother especially when she remarried after her father passed away. Her step father cared for her in a kind and generous way despite her utter indifference toward him. When her half brother was born, Anne took no special interest in the boy and held that attitude toward him until he found a job and bought a boat after he had left home. When the brother moved to Severna Park and began work in a machine shop, she let him take her out on the Bay though she initiated the idea. These weekend excursions would last most of a Saturday for trips to Harris's on Kent Narrows for crabs. Since both were taciturn to a fault, few words passed between them save for directions to tie up or agreeing on the crab size order. They held good feelings for one another but rarely spoke on the boat or in the restaurant. The parents were never invited. She did love the water as did the brother. While similar in so many ways, no regular communication existed between them especially in months when no Bay crabs were available. When spring arrived however, she would drive him down to Crisfield to visit their aunt who had a mysterious connection with several watermen. The aunt would prepare them soft shelled crabs in the same recipe they had known as children. She would brush eight dressed jumbo soft shell crabs with a paste of two tablespoons of melted butter and three tablespoons of brown deli mustard. When the outdoor grill was hot she'd char each side for two minutes each. Even the hardened watermen in Crisfield lined up at her cottage in season.

While there for long weekends, Anne took the day cruises alone over to Smith Island and Tangier Island. On the return trips to the mainland she pondered if she would be content with a lifestyle much removed from her own and decided she could. Were she to move one day, an island or peninsula on the Bay would be her choice. Being on or surrounded by the water pleased her so favorably that small plans to that end had entered her consciousness. Kent Island and Tilghman Island held her preference. For then however, she loved Annapolis as much or more than anything in her life.

In reality, Anne had no close friends. No amount of compassion in her prompted a desire to be close to any woman friend. Many acquaintances tried to warm up to her and establish friendship but in vain. The awful truth began with deceit or at least insincerity bordering on gross deception. Her mother had always instilled the idea of 'choose your own friends, don't let them choose you.' These women, who avowed their fealty to Anne, meant to use her for their own best advantage. They needed her place to 'crash' after bar hopping in Annapolis, needed her to accompany them to a bar as a 'puller' so they could pick from all the men she attracted or simply needed to be in the company of a dynamic, beautiful woman. She became even more suspicious of the latter because they were interested more in her than men she attracted. Anne found most women meddlesome and most men impertinent. Evenings at home alone held no loneliness for her. As time passed she preferred her own company. Saturdays evenings marked her only excursions into society from a gala at a grand hotel in Washington to steamed crabs at Cantler's Riverside Inn on Mill Creek, preferably by boat. In fact, she preferred the crabs. If an event, invitation or gathering proffered itself on any other night she politely refused on the grounds that she was indisposed which she wasn't. As she grew more insular, she grew more content. If the notion struck, a pleasant stroll on warm evenings found her at the city dock or in Eastport for a singular light supper. The carefree bustle and business of her town pleased her temperate, appreciating nature. The tourists, locals and boaters mingled with college students and midshipmen against the boats and water views of which she never tired. She enjoyed watching people enjoying themselves and knew her pleasure to be spoiled were she to participate.

Many fine Fridays found her taking a morning cruise on the 'Woodwind,' the three mast schooner docked at Pusser's Caribbean Grill at the Marriott waterfront hotel. On Monday evenings she would take the sunset cruise which took tourists out on the Bay for the glorious settings. They also sailed up the Severn to the bridge. She never tired of these views of the Academy and her hometown. Not often, but not rarely either, Anne would bump into acquaintances whose invitation that evening she had spurned by feigned illness or out of town travel to avoid their company. After suffering only the mildest rebukes from them, she promised acceptance at their next little soiree which she had no intention of honoring were it on any other time but a Saturday. Even then, the chances were slim; a year only containing fifty-two opportunities of her gracing the invitation. No embarrassment affected her as she resumed her promenade. She just didn't care.

Since, as the new office manager, duties required her to open the office by eight o'clock, Anne arrived each morning at seven-thirty. She made preparations for any internal meetings, listed directions for the support staff and updated the major partners on any last minute changes regarding court appearances, conferences and appointments. In bed by nine on most nights Anne loved the old movies on television. She preferred the plots, storylines and the actors' character portrayals. Maybe the attraction to a bygone era of entertainment held her fascination. She didn't know. She had blossomed in the disco era and detested it. The horrible clothes, men's bell bottomed vest suits worn over some brightly colored paisley shirt with wide dog ear collars, ballooned sleeves, and unbuttoned to the waist prevented her from dating and going to clubs more than she could have. She detested the music and dancing of the era. The men wore twice the jewelry of the women and the platform shoes they wore were higher than her high heels; they 'permed' their hair and wore mustaches which she detested.

As much as she liked to dress well, only polyester dresses and pant suits were available to her limited budget and she loathed the feel of the unnatural, inorganic material. The period clothing of the older movies had set a unconscious standard of dress for her. She had hoped at times that women's fashion might return to sensible tastes. By the early nineties she realized her wish for the 'beauty in simplicity' ideal with classic cuts and fine fabrics had been answered. She hopefully felt that she may never have to survive another 'Russian peasant look' season again.

By the start of the last decade of the century Anne had been thriving in the computer age. Self trained for the most part, she was sent by her forward looking firm to any I.T. tutorials she deemed necessary for the advanced instruction. Beyond her office duties she had initiated, installed, instructed and infused the company with the most cutting edge technology. Her work load, now double from ten years ago, called for all the multi-tasking gifts she possessed. The partners often remarked that she would make a great attorney. Save for the years it would demand for an undergraduate degree and law school, all part time and at night, they were secretly happy she wasn't a lawyer. They were constantly adding new attorneys to the practice. They were a dime a dozen. Anne was irreplaceable. The intangible profitability she brought to the firm out weighed the revenue of any five new advocates; and she was compensated accordingly. The turn of the century brought more but pleasing and profitable work to her and a once in a lifetime dilemma. The Annapolis firm she had fed, nurtured, baby sat and reared had grown to some distinct prominence in the Capital and made Anne an offer for her permanent services. The two nascent attorneys had blossomed into a powerful law firm representing some of the largest companies in the state. They were lobbyists. In the beginning they relied on Anne to teach them to file an action and what cases and clients they should take on or avoid. As desperate as they were for business in the early days, the freshly minted lawyers bowed to her experience and were the better for it. She had sat in too many conferences and meetings and listened to the expertise of her employers not to have noted what types of prospective clients were bums, deadbeats and cases not worth the trouble. When unsure about a problem her guys in Annapolis were having, she'd simply consult one or more of the partners for their counsel which they readily gave and knowing for whom it was meant.

Two reasons prompted her decision to stay and neither derived from a true sense of loyalty. Anne actually liked the commute straight into D.C. Being alone with her music and audio books gave her pleasure twice daily in her beloved sport sedan which she still maintained. She liked being alone. The second, and to her as important, her present firm was national and fried bigger fish; the local firm only state wide. Since the stakes were higher she remained. After informing her firm that she was considering the change and talking to the Maryland group, her old partners showed their appreciation of her frankness and honesty. When announcing her decision to stay, their gratitude announced itself a week later when the HR department called to say an envelope awaited her. The check to her read one hundred thousand dollars.

With an ever increasing savings, Anne had all her assets tied up in cash. From money market accounts to certificates of deposit, she forsook any other types of investments. Yet for reasons she couldn't explain to herself she found little consolation in the amount she'd accrued in the bank and retirement plans. Only adding to her capital balance every month and making generous donations anonymously to charities related to cleaning up and saving the Bay gave her any pleasure. She had a ravenous appetite for well prepared dishes especially the seasonal seafood of the Bay. Real crab cakes, fresh unwashed oysters, crabs cooked to order and rock fish which she still called striped bass from her childhood topped her list. Occasionally she'd attend a dinner with neighbors but only if she knew beforehand that the 'cook' that evening had passed her sample test. Always well received by her hosts, she made a delightful addition to any dinner party. They used her to dress up their usually drab guest list and alleviate the predictable ennui which smoldered in the dining room after the meal. She used them for the tastily prepared dishes and well made balanced, expensive wines they poured. Were she asked out to dinner, Anne considered the quality of the escort through an excoriating examination of his looks, personality, propriety and his ability to pay for what she knew would be a fine meal with wine. Annapolis had grown in population along with the number of finer restaurants since she became a resident all those years ago.

At first she regarded internet dating as an extremely dangerous proposition for both genders. When cyber based dating services began advertising and guaranteeing arduous screening and publicized their results, Anne, ever the skeptic, delved into company's claims and results. After thorough and lengthy investigation, she decided to try it one time. Her brother came from Severna Park to take portrait photos of her. She didn't glamorize herself for beauty shots or doll up any more than normal. Her dark hair had shone just the slightest hint of grey and she had it professionally colored a few times since she noticed the change. In her late forties, which she related on her personal profile form in perfect honesty, she was still a very attractive woman. In a moment of sheer vanity she signaled on her vital 'stats' that her nickname was Annie for the youthfulness of its sound. Another reason egged her on in this pursuit. She had rather run through by several times all her known local dinner partners. She began to find their conversation and company discursive and tiresome. The dates, all successful men she had met or known through the law practices, at first were whimsical and fanciful, all attempting to woo her into bed. After about three expensive meals with each, their attitude became brusque if not shirty. Anne suffered their displeasures with her. She didn't care as long as the food was delicious and the wine to her standards. The final blow of her dinner dating rotation came, when after four very good meals with her favorite benefactor, he suggested that she treat at their next repast. She never spoke to or saw him again. Almost out of necessity she had to take her chances online.

Her first cyber date turned out to be a gentle, kind, slightly built engineer from Aberdeen who was chosen for no other reason than he liked to eat well and asked her to recommend a restaurant in Annapolis. They met at the restaurant, maybe her favorite. The date could only be counted as highly delightful. Not only did he not attempt to impress her with his attributes but attended to his surf and turf as ardently as she did her stuffed rockfish. After a polite good night and the hope that the two would reprise the evening, Annie mulled the idea and decided to put the engineer on a repeat list. As seasons ended and began and for as many Saturday night rendezvous dinners with strangers she'd accepted, not one had bordered on impropriety. She now had her choice of a dozen men in her rota. While they may have considered themselves suitors, in truth they were only a source of free meals to her. As before for years, Annie sat home on work nights eating cold cereal with fruit in bed. Propped up with three pillows, she watched old movies usually in black and white. She abhorred Ted Turner for colorizing the great classics. She had taken to buying these movies when they came on sale. Otherwise, she would have to watch that drivel that Hollywood was producing for the last thirty years. Her cut off date was 1985. She could recall on one hand the films that pleased her after that year. She liked looking at a young Brad Pitt, a Johnny Depp or a 'Top Gun' Tom Cruise but she generally watched their works while the remote was on mute. She didn't mind looking at Angelina Jolie, Scarlett Johansson or Kiera Knightly either. No, Cary Grant and Irene Dunn were the standard to which all actors and actresses should be held and she didn't like women who called themselves 'actors.' She had never viewed a film with a lot of special effects.

After being a loyal employee for the last three decades she continued to work but only six hours a day with Fridays off. Anything that needed her attention could be dealt with through her iPhone or her home office set up by her and paid for by the firm. She looked forward to Saturday night and the good meal that it promised. Her consort for the coming evening would be a second timer who said he loved the trendy, wonderful steak place in Eastport. Which one she asked herself, Lewnes, Ruth's Chris, she could go on. At least she knew it wouldn't be the seafood bistro near city dock where the maitre d' knew her only too well because she appeared regularly, sometimes with different dates, sometimes with the same. The sycophant greeter had taken to the habit lately of giving her the fish eye, smirking knowingly only whenever their glances met. He would slowly slide the dinner napkin as she sat, dragging it more below her waist than across her lap. He seemed to happen by her table to chat her up only while her date was in the restroom. Maybe he could give her a pretty good discount or even a free meal if she came alone. The napkin placing was a little fresh. Oh well, she didn't care. A girl's gotta eat.

❖ ❖ ❖ ⛵ ❖ ❖ ❖

TENNIS BALL BEACH

B y the time they arrived at the Vet's office, Millie had sat up
again. She knew where she was. The early hour had begun
to lose its struggle with the approaching summer sun rising
quickly from the middle of the eastern shore. Even with all the
windows down and the open sun roof, Tim had the A/C on full
blast as was his custom on mornings and evenings in the summer
for their rides to the park or the beach. He left no windows open
during the day though, when she was allowed to tag along this
time of year. The cold forced air from the sleek, new BMW 7
Series permitted her to accompany Tim only when he had the
shortest of errands, usually drive-through journeys to the bank
or pharmacy The pliable leather back seat to which Millie had
accustomed herself while returning home from the dealership
the day Tim traded his six year old model in, removed any fear
he may have had about her yearning for her former car. He
bought the car for her. The Black Lab now took in the smells in

the ground outside Dr. Karas' office. After a parade around the freshly mown field, she limply guided Tim to the front door which was locked. Nick Karas was coming into his office at ten o'clock on Sunday just to re-examine her and go over all the biopsy results and blood work. Millie had been the doctor's first canine patient when he opened his small practice twelve years earlier; a fluffy gold Tabby with the 'sniffles' had the very first appointment and beat Millie out for the honor of first over-all patient. During normal visits she assumed a pose of slight superiority around the other pets in the waiting room if only because of the preponderance of affiliation with the Vet. Technicians had come and gone but the doctor and the redolence of the area and the office itself remained. Tim held that her remarkable beauty became unnoticed when people acquainted themselves with her gentle spirit and fetching personality. Of course he knew all dogs and cats were regarded with the same love and esteem by their proud owners. He had met many Labs, black, yellow, chocolate and mixed and the shaggiest of them all to him were still beautiful and well tempered.

Tim had found Millie in a pound in Harford County when she was six months old. He had lost his wife in a boating accident on the Bay the previous summer when she and her two friends went sailing, got caught in an unexpected thunder storm and capsized. She was the only fatality and found three days later. No alcohol had been found in her body and had not been a contributing factor. There were no other boating mishaps on the upper Bay that afternoon and in the end it was determined an accident, caused by an act of nature. The shock had never abated and he retired from his work as a manager at Bethlehem Steel and later Martin Marietta. He had never been a 'pet' man since he grew up in Dundalk, Maryland in one of the thousands of row houses that surrounded St. Rita's parish. Some older neighbors on Cornwall Avenue kept a cat or two but few dogs were known to the blue collar neighborhood. After attending Dundalk Elementary, Dundalk Junior and Dundalk Senior High School he left for The University of Maryland in College Park. He became homesick and took his degree in Business Administration from a lesser known college closer to home and started work as a professional making one third his father's wages at the same plant. His father had not been schooled past the eighth grade. Tim had been smitten by a girl from the neighborhood whom he had always liked but never knew well until he knocked a box of popcorn and a Coke all over her at one of the local drive-in theater's concession stands. She was shopping for her pouty boyfriend who remained in the car so he wouldn't miss any of the Zorro serial or coming attractions. Tim was with three friends, two of whom were smuggled into the starlit theater in the trunk of his Chevy Impala. He apologized profusely to this very pretty girl as he attempted to pat dry with napkins the Coke soaked sweater until he realized, to his horror, that he actually was rubbing the napkins very smoothly over her very firm breasts. They wed at St. Rita's four months later. The childless marriage brought no unhappiness to either one, just tacit mutual consolation borne from true love. They would have made very good parents. Because of this deprivation an even deeper closeness and bond arose between them akin to couples who love each other more because of the love of their children.

Dr. Karas came from the back where the consulting rooms and surgery were to let them in. His greeting to them was not forced with pretended pleasure but the man's façade attempted no disguise about the gravity of Millie's results. As a puppy she had been battered and kicked by the ten and twelve year old sons of the owner who left her in shock and pain at the animal rescue's front door on his way to work. It was determined by the staff, when they arrived to open and found her, that she must be euthanized that day. She was already sedated, caged and awaiting her doom with a half a dozen other dogs whom no one had rescued in the prescribed time allowed by law. Tim arrived by chance. He had spent the night with old friends in Belair. The couple held a small dinner party and there was no mistaking their attempt at a 'fix-up' between Tim and a very attractive and intelligent divorcee. He liked the woman well enough and knew that after a year of being widowed his general state of mind had returned, his life would go on, and only small reminisces of the past occasionally welled up in a still broken heart. So as much for Millie as for Tim did fate allow him to stop at the shelter on his way home the next morning. He accepted the very cordial greeting from the staff. It takes some passion to care for abandoned and abused animals as a job and they were always made happy if an animal were adopted. They showed him a lively group of mostly young dogs of mixed breed and he liked them all. He thought that how hard it would be for him to choose one over the others.

Then he saw Millie. Inquiring about her, he was told her condition; a shattered femur and fractured hip. Only costly surgeries and a miracle could save her; the staff was insistent that he not adopt her. She was nearly hopeless and had also shown the first signs of mange. He paid the fee, promised to spay her if she survived and left a donation uncommon in recent memory. He wrapped her in his old yellow sailing jacket from the trunk of his car. Her bones had protruded through her frail, under nourished frame and the well worn but sturdy three quarter length Nautica coat. Tim intended to save her and Dr. Karas did save her indeed. After two operations, a year of therapy, kindness and attention, follow up visits and patience by both men, the Lab not only survived but flourished. Her main recommended rehabilitation was lengthy swimming which was like prescribing ice cream to children after a tonsillectomy. In the summer Tim and Millie would visit the Vet and his wife on their large waterfront but modest home at Sparrows Point. After crabbing in the morning with Millie, the two men returned to cook the crabs. Tim would allow her to jump in and swim the last hundred yards beside the boat to the dock. Nick said it was the best thing for her. Dr. Karas anointed himself a genius with the black crab pot.

While he and Tim picked crabs, pausing only to pull two cans of 'Natty Bohs' from an aluminum tub chocked with ice and beer, Millie laid under the table and stared back at the fury black once feral cat the Doc's wife insist they keep when she found him living at the marina in the middle of winter. While suspicious of each other, Millie and Tommy certainly possessed some type of mutual respect. Dr. Karas explained the phenomenon and dynamic to Tim as professionally as he could and then threw his hands up declaring maybe because he and Tim were such friends the animals that lived with and depended on them should be so as well.

Every day after breakfast, barring very inclement weather, she waited for Tim to announce, "Get your tennis ball. Do you want to go to the beach? Get your tennis ball. C'mon. We'll go to the beach."

Snatching her leash from the banister and sprinting at an unsafe speed from the kitchen to Tim's small library to a basket of assorted old stuffed animals and tennis balls, Millie reacted with the same daily exuberance as if she were a trained actress playing a well rehearsed role on stage. Often while chasing the ball thrown by Tim out on the Bay, Millie would espy a few ducks just sitting on the water minding their own business. Forgoing the tennis ball, her instinct directed her to wade out to fetch these un-amused fowl, put them gently in her mouth, return them to shore and drop them at Tim's feet. By her nature she assumed that these sitting ducks had been successfully hunted. It was then her job to fetch and return. When Millie arrived in their vicinity the ducks would offer her a tiresome glance and merely paddle quickly away. Tim would give her an old fashioned Dundalk ribbing when she returned. Her response to this laughing abuse was to shake gallons of Bay water on him at close range. His delight matched hers and they settled into a routine which was neither ordinary nor routine. They loved each other.

"Tim, the results aren't good. Her platelets are still low, the 'Pred.' isn't working anymore and she's losing all back end strength. Full Dysplasia is probably days, not weeks, away. How did she do last night?"

"O.K., considering."

"How low did you have the A/C?"

"Sixty."

"The mass on her chest is not going to do her in but I told you her breathing will get worse."

"When's the time?"

"Today, Tim, now. You know that's why I had you come this morning. I know you don't want her to suffer. She's had a great life because of you."

"No, Nick, it's the reverse."

The veterinarian looked away briefly. He had become inured to these situations but every so often the pain and loss of the owners moved him at these times. This was different and never had his sympathy been so moved for the person and the animal. The Vet's own sorrow overcame his professional demeanor. Millie and Tim were his friends. The black lab always received a treat from the big fish bowl on the counter after her visits. Nick left the room where Millie laid beside Tim who noticed the room was freezing. When he returned, he stooped with four treats in the palm of his hand. She lapped them slowly as if taking communion.

After the sedation and final injection, Millie died. Tim carried her out of the office which had saved then taken her life. Tim and Nick had parted with no words; just a knowing and understanding that only certain men have in time of peril and great unhappiness. In the trunk Tim wrapped her in the same yellow sea worn jacket in which he had brought her home from the pound and laid her gently on the back seat, her back seat. When their bodies washed ashore at Sparrow's Point near Bear Creek, Millie and Tim were zipped in the jacket with her cheek on his shoulder.

❖ ❖ ❖ ⛵ ❖ ❖ ❖

THE CHOPTANK CHUM*P

When the three modern SUVs left the parking lot at four A.M. to make the excursion from Timonium to Cambridge, each member but one, had a thermos jug of home brewed coffee cupped between their palms. The driver had to be content to set his insulated stainless steel mug in the console's cup holder. The other drank a small cup of hot tea from the 7/11. What bonded most of the group of twelve men was the annual trek to the Eastern Shore for two days of duck hunting and serious but somewhat controlled eating and drinking. Save for the newcomer, the other eleven were avid hunters who had more or less grown up fishing and hunting with fathers, uncles and brothers even if they did not live in rural areas but most had. This became the sixth trip for the proprietor of the real estate investment firm and each season the party grew until the anointed dozen remained the same for the past three Novembers. With four to a vehicle the same proportion would be assigned to small head boats the next morning when the hunting party would venture from Knapp's Narrows onto the Bay in frigid temperatures an hour before sun up which approximated very nearly the amount of darkness in which they travelled to their destination now. Today they would reach the farm of a successful client who had purchased the hundreds of acres on the Choptank River for the bucolic atmosphere of his childhood. While he subsidized the tenant farmers he hired to bring in the crops, the main benefits to this scion of land investments were purely for the hunting and fishing it provided him and his friends, not to mention the inestimable tax relief it garnered for him every April 15th.

By the time the caffeine fueled conversation waned, the caravan pulled into the fishing and hunting emporium, Anglers, near the Bay Bridge. There was no need for bait or tackle. They descended on the store for one thing, ammo, shot gun shells by the box loads. Ward, the young neophyte, couldn't believe at how early the store opened or that they were doing a brisk business at six A.M. Of the two hundred employees of his firm, these eleven were the chosen few. They were the top producers, the 'hired guns.' The head honcho selected the group which he favored mainly because they were like him by nature or affectation. A few other men at the office could have been in this select cadre except for the clash of temperament. No women ever found themselves on the hunting trips but the top producers among them were treated as royally as their male counterparts on the company sponsored February excursions to warm-climate exotic resorts. No, this was a 'guy's' thing and the women agents were just as happy to have most of this group out of the office for a few days. Of course the support staff, male or female, was never invited. Well catered, company sponsored picnics and Christmas parties and nice bonuses easily soothed any pretended hard feelings. The owner paid top dollar for top talent, offered generous leave policies, matching retirement contributions and compensated a large portion of the best dental and health care coverage. In all, the work lent itself to a hectic yet congenial work environment for all those who functioned successfully and performed their jobs well. Slackers, buffoons, and liability risks would not be brooked by the owner and found themselves impertinently and hastily severed with cause from the company. The stakes were as high as the competition was tough but at the end of the day the firm stood, without contradiction, as the most successful in town.

At eight thirty the caravan pulled into Cambridge. The family style restaurant sat at a crossroads where many bird hunters in the region had converged after the break of day shooting. The camouflaged gathering breakfasted in quiet during a lull between the morning and afternoon hunt. Evinced by the three day growths, they tacitly acknowledged Ward's group as a new hunting party arriving on their first day. A pleasantly plump waitress with a mass of yellow curls stacked atop her head capped with a black adornment, which could only be described as a hat, caught their eye. 'De rigueur', for food handlers, the black satin cap was no larger than a small bow tie. She breezed by the newcomers in a flurry with a smile and a mission. Holding four platters of eggs, pancakes, waffles, scrapple sausage, thick rashers of crispy bacon and loaves of toast, she motioned with a tilt and exaggerated nod of her head toward the only three remaining four top tables scattered through the dining room. The gesture, made without stopping or without a strand of hair moving out of its chemically assigned place, seemed a marvel of balance and dexterity. She openly winked and in a happy voice, "Seat yourselves, hon."

Even the novice, Ward, reflected that comfortable countenance that bespoke familiarity as he and his co-workers ambled in and sat at the open tables. To the young Ward, no safety in numbers instilled any confidence as he sat with his car pool. He felt unaware that he, his boss and buddies had passed the subtle eye ball test of the room but they knew of the mute acceptance even if he didn't. Had he entered a club or a pool hall in North Baltimore, he would have understood better.

When they reached the 'farm house' several miles down the Choptank River, after following a meandering lane off the state road, Ward imagined at first that the large white home that he espied would be his quarters for the next two nights. When they pulled up in front of the main house, invisible from down the lane because of the wide but barren elms and oaks that guarded the gravelly path, he was he informed that the other building served as quarters for the keepers of the grounds. Three men awaited them on the veranda of the ante-bellum mansion, then showed the way to the bedrooms upstairs. Five rooms held four beds ranging from a king size and three singles in the master and a combination of doubles and singles in the others. The renovated home seemed to Ward that its architects had remodeled the home for the very purpose for which it now served, a glorified bunk house. With an hour to kill before the afternoon shooting, Ward strolled through the well decorated rooms then to the rear porches and back grounds and gardens. The straw colored lawn led past the tennis court and covered swimming pool down to a boatless dock which seemed to him to be able to comfortably accommodate several crafts of some size in warm weather. Ward walked the length of the pier which jutted out thirty yards from the shore. The wide, flowing Choptank underneath gave him the sensation of being on a boat and it pleased him. He had passed through Cambridge so many times on his way to Ocean City and never gave a thought to the town or its environs. Now the notion of discovery stimulated him to find out more about its history and the broad river upon which it sat. Driving out of town after breakfast, he had tried to notice the direction and landmarks for future reference. Once through the picture postcard homes in town, he'd guessed their direction must be west for the position of the weak sun struggling to pierce the mid November sky. An echoing shout broke his reverie as he stared across the graceful river. The entire hunting party clamored about on the front portico while they chastised him for not being prepared.

"C'mon Ward, were ready to roll."

Only then did he realize that everyone had changed into gear resembling those at the restaurant and he looked completely estranged from these men in hunting boots, hunting jackets and hunting hats. Dashing upstairs to change, he realized something that put him in a temporary fit of disgust. He abhorred detaining people or making anyone wait for him. Two days before the trip he had spent hundreds of dollars at a sporting goods store on the items they had told him to purchase. He had brought the gear still in the store bags, rolled up and stuffed in a duffle bag along with the new boots. Delving into the bag, the mass of garments appeared to him as a jigsaw puzzle. In a panic to separate all the clothing into the sequence and order required, he realized he hadn't even taken his jeans, sweater and tennis shoes off yet. Another roadblock reared when he saw that he hadn't taken the sales tags, labels and consumer care tags off any item. They seemed to be several on each piece of inner and outerwear riveted to the items by a plastic stapling gun for which he had no tool to remove them. The location of all these impedimenta differed from piece to piece in places on the garments that were as various as they were curious. Again a shouting demand from outside to him in more astringent language that he understood only too well only exacerbated his dilemma. Stiffening to the challenge, he uttered to himself, 'Haste makes waste' and began to succeed with the dressing. As he ran down the spiral staircase carrying the boots with the unique lacing contrived and tied by the manufacturer and the wads of tan tissue paper erupting from the open tops, he jolted and slid in his socks to a most abrupt stop. While passing the large gilt edged mirror in the foyer he had espied an accidental glimpse of himself. Not wanting to dally another second, he ruefully retreated to the antique looking glass for a sight of mortification itself. His immediate thoughts were two; 'The Michelin Tire Man' or worse, 'The Pillsbury Dough Boy.' He modestly knew that no one in the company dressed or wore their clothes any better than he. He took pride in his wardrobe on a personal and business level. Clients, women and men, liked to do business with associates who appeared well appointed and he had always 'dressed for success.' Why then didn't he look like the rest of the guys instead of a figure, were his outfit white instead of green, that resembled a snowman constructed by children on too much sugar and caffeine?

As he slithered into the back seat, the goose down stuffed rayon outfit left hardly any room for his back seat passenger who remarked, "Hey Ward, do you have any all weather radials for a Lexus 400?"

His mercurial ascension into the elite 'club' had taken less than a year. He had been in direct competition with the top producer of his new company for five years. His reputation as a diligent, tough but friendly account manager grew from the clients who preferred to work with him rather than his competitor. In addition Ward had a stable of clients who were constantly being wooed by this adversary whose nickname, outside and in his own company, because of his propensity to wear the same suit coat with three utterly unmatched pairs of slacks, was 'Same Suit Sam.' Although Sam never flustered when colleagues exaggerated his thriftiness, being the tightwad in this altogether frugal group didn't serve him well. The C.E.O., Angelo, the head man and leader, who spread the wealth when it was there to be spread, often excoriated Sam for his meanness. Sam contributed to the firm's bottom line as well as his own based on the attributes necessary for a man to be highly successful in the world of business. He was tall, middle aged, a bachelor and good looking. Sam also possessed a mane of thick, shiny, silver and black hair that enticed women's fingers and tempted them at the chance to run their hands through its sleekness. It mattered little that he had no male clients, he didn't need them.

So it was ten months previous when the call came from Angelo and his lieutenant, Sal, a youngish, military type with a quick smile and a no nonsense attitude. Through an intermediary, an appointment only to meet came as no surprise to Ward. While in the well decorated lobby, Ward noticed a preponderance of *Field and Stream* issues on the cherry wood tables. No *Sports Illustrated*, *Time*, and certainly no *Vanity Fair*.

When greeted by Angelo and ushered into the paneled conference room for their meeting, Ward pretended not to be shocked by Angelo's appearance. He had known of him since he entered the business right out of school but the two had never met. Tan, athletic and slender, under a mop of long blond hair, Angelo seemed out of place anywhere east of Hawaii. His youth may have been the most surprising aspect since he appeared no older than Ward who needed to celebrate two more birthdays to enter his third decade of life. The man who held the firm hand shake between the two for an extra half second, pierced Ward's eyes with globular brown eyes as if making an attempt to stare through him. Accidently smiling at the notion, he asked Ward, "What, did I say something funny?"

"No, you hadn't said anything yet. You did something funny. You squeezed my hand a little longer than necessary and then attempted to stare right through me. I wasn't laughing but it did make me smile."

At this, Sal, then Angelo laughed facing each other.

"That's good, that's real good. Is that how you act on job interviews?"

"Am I on a job interview?"

"I guess it wasn't exactly described that way but now that you're here, what do you think? You work for a national company. They're uptight and awkward in this market place. Everything they do, every decision they make has to come from their corporate headquarters wherever that is. It's got to come down the pike. We're not small though and only operate in Maryland. In fact we're bigger in Maryland than they are. You see me and Sal? We are the pike. Everything comes from us."

At that, both executives took business cards from their shirt pockets and placed them on the mahogany conference table in front of Ward.

"Joplin."

"Joplin, what's 'Joplin'? What the hell does that mean exactly?"

"Joplin, Missouri; it's where our corporate headquarters are located."

"Tell me something Sal, does it feel like were the ones being interviewed?"

"Maybe we are, Angelo."

"We know what clients you could bring on board. They stay with you."

"Angelo, I compete with Sam on the other third of my business. I don't think he'll take kindly to me calling on the same clients."

"Don't worry about Sam. Ward, do you like to hunt; birds, ducks, big game?"

"I don't know."

"You don't know. How could you not know?"

"I've never been hunting."

"Have you ever fired a gun? Where are you from?"

"I'm from Baltimore City. No, I've never fired a gun but I've been in a few knife fights. Does that count?"

"Jeez Sal, do believe this guy? Well all my top guys here hunt. We'll have to teach you. Sal will take care of you."

With another firm but less pronounced hand shake, he was gone. He's probably going back to his office to wax down his surfboard, Ward thought.

"What were you thinking in terms of signing bonus, expense account and car?"

"Sal, I want it all but what I need is the ability to make a deal that's on the verge of going the other way unless we give something up. It's fine to get clients to know you, like you and trust you but if we lose their deals for fifty dollars or fifty thousand, they never come back. I consider it an investment in their future business."

"You're coming to the right place. Angelo will do a deal for no income if you're willing to do the same. We have a few people here who want us to take the entire hit but they want to get paid full boat."

"Same Suit Sam?"

"Bingo."

"What's next?"

"See you next Monday. Do you want to know something? Angelo's from southern Missouri."

The acreage they drove to, located a few miles from the lodge abutted hard on a creek that led into the Little Choptank River. No large home here only fallow fields which seemed endless in three directions save for the water. Ward could see what looked to be duck blinds on certain corners of the property slightly masked by a sparse tree line. There were a couple of blinds built on poles sitting a hundred yards into the creek. The land huts appeared to be about a quarter of a mile apart. He didn't know what to do, where to go or what to ask. The conundrum solved itself after all the guns were unloaded from the backs of the vehicles. A gathering crowded around him; all with sheepish grins. Angelo pulled him to the center and made a congratulatory reference to Ward's production year to date and especially his numbers for the recently ended third quarter. With another firm gripping of hands, Angelo took a finely carved and lacquered box from Sal then presented it to Ward accompanied by some rather brief, muffled but genuine applause from twenty-two insulated gloves. Inside, the Beretta over and under shot gun looked more a trophy than the beautifully imported weapon nestled stoically inside its sculptured, velvet cradle. Angelo's words were brief but sounded well meant.

"Ward, you've done a great job since you started without stepping on anyone's toes here, which is hard to do in this industry. Plus, we are all so happy to see you in that get-up. Sal, please get a picture for blackmail purposes."

"Thank you, everyone."

At that Angelo pulled Ward with him and two men whom he knew to be experienced outdoorsmen and headed up a dirt road that separated two large fields. When they reached the blind near the water, Ward looked back and had lost sight of the others. As best he could, he determined they must be at least a quarter of a mile from the cars. On the way the three men began giving him instructions and lessons, usually their own styles and preferences for bringing down the quarry. This counsel was all well and good except the basic mechanics of his unloaded gun, now in a chamois skinned sheath hanging down over his right forearm, was a mystery to him. The constant thought that pervaded his mind rested firmly on the one topic, safety. He refused to allow the word accident into his concentrated self disciplined inner discussion. He might have been a bit more affable about receiving such a gift when he was presented his award but kept it short and hoped no one thought him ungrateful because of it. One, he knew the guys wanted to get at whatever the day entailed and he didn't want to delay them more than he already had; two, he had begun a gushing sweat on the short ride from all the layers of thermal, lined, insulated and downed attire he had swathed himself in.

Dying of thirst, he couldn't sate his dehydrated body until the gear was unloaded at his new home for the next two hours. Once they had situated themselves in what was more like a manger, his mates showed him how to load the shot gun. He was allowed one shell at a time and was assured this was the pattern for all novices which suited him just fine. Without asking, his mates told Ward that just a few decoys had been set in the water behind the blinds. His post on the corner of the open blind would be his area and he was only to fire at his target within a thirty degree angle starting at thirty feet. For insurance Angelo stood next to him and told Ward two main rules; his gun should always be reloaded with the barrel facing downwards over the counter high opening of the blind and never cross barrels with his neighbor to get a shot. Besides, his boss would direct the novice when and at what to shoot, which was also fine with Ward. For practice he let Ward fire two shells in the air which approximated the intended flight of his victims. Even at that he had a hard time hitting his assigned open space. The comment in the blind was if he were aiming in his area and were it geometrically extended ad infinitum and missed both times, he might want to attempt to stone the fowl to death. The first shot was loosed too low and the second too wide. Only because he had become a great source of amusement did he feel comfortable for the first time. The three hunters expected little of him and he expected even less. After an hour and a half nothing appeared in the air. The men ate the sandwiches prepared for them by keepers back at the main house, talked a little business then fell silent. In fact, Ward perceived an embarrassing quietude which he owed to the absence of the un-cooperating water fowl. Still, it was not yet noon.

A lapping of small waves behind them lulled Ward into a daydream. The early rising, brisk breeze off the water and crisp cold air combined with inactivity gave pause to a fitful energy he had felt all morning. With his back to the rest he peered out the shutterless side of the shelter. His gaze held no one object but a spectrum of sights not so interesting on their own but embroidered together the scene, bathed in the faint light of late autumn, captured and held his attention. Bare limbs of a distant tree line that guarded a dense copse stood up as the back drop of the sallow, barren fields which ran up to their ancient trunks. He had never cared for or had ever been exposed to the outdoors. He didn't ski, hike or bicycle. He had played sports as a teenager but gave them up after high school for golf on well manicured courses in fine weather. He had flirted with a brief surfing infatuation in college which he pursued mostly to attract girls. A true urchin of the inner city, he had had no contact with the fishermen or hunters and knew no one who did; until now.

So mesmerizing, so indefinable was his reverie of this simple landscape at this time of year that he couldn't grasp the whole idea of it. When his spell was broken, it was by a voice replete with disappointment and resignation.

"Pack up. Let's go."

No ducks had come.

Instead of asking about the proposed agenda for the balance of the day and tomorrow's schedule he followed the group's conversations to pick up any useful information which would prevent any tardiness again. A good deal came from Sam who spoke often and rather mostly to himself even in a crowd.

"I'm hitting the bunk 'til happy hour. I can't keep up with these flat bellies anymore especially if we have to be at the bridge to Tilghman Island at six A.M. Besides, I'm looking forward to that dinner tonight and who knows how late that'll last. No, Sammy needs his beauty rest. Night, night sweet prince."

Before he realized it, the expansive kitchen in which they had all congregated to commiserate about the luckless morning had emptied. Ward wanted to make another promenade around the grounds including revisiting the long boat dock on the Choptank at the bottom of the sprawling back lawn to continue his musings but thought better of the idea. He lay down on his bed just to rest his eyes. His three roomies were already fast asleep and snoring mildly. How, he wondered, would he be able to take a nap at two o'clock in the afternoon? He realized he wasn't dreaming, when that same familiar raucous voice which had chastised him twice already that morning, boomed in with an echoing fusillade of mirthful abuse.

"C'mon on Ward, get up. Are you going to sleep all day?"

Aware that he wasn't asleep then, he staggered almost drunkenly to the bathroom warmed by steam from the just used shower which had also befogged the mirrors. Glancing at a clock on a night table he stiffened and caught himself between shock and disbelief. Could it be four-thirty? He hopped on one leg as he pulled on his jeans and hastened toward the banter and laughter below stairs. He found the source of the agreeable mirth and bonhomie in the spacious dining room. It originated from eleven freshly showered, shaved and casually but country elegantly dressed men who turned their immediate attention on Ward as he stumbled into the room which went silent. Only then, through the support of yet another ornately framed mirror, did it appear as if a bedraggled, unshaven intruder wearing one woolen sock, perspiration stained thermal under shirt, crumpled dungarees and a shock of electric hair had foisted itself upon these civilized gentlemen. The suddenness of his interruption silenced the men who were in the process of decanting bottles of '97, '98 and '99 Chateau Lafite, a vertical of classic vintages from Angelo's famous home wine cellar. Sam, who held the lit candle under the neck of the second vessel for that step in the ritual, proceeded after the slightest of hesitations only to utter, "Hey Ward, your fly's down."

Joining in the hilarity, Ward sheepishly retreated for a hot shower, dressed and returned to the kitchen which held two modern refrigerators, one chocked with food, the other brimming with bottles of Budweiser, Bud Lite and Miller Lite. Opening a tall neck Bud, he joined the wine tasting ceremony which proceeded without him. On seeing Ward, Angelo shook his head.

"Put that beer down. These are your three glasses and water. You've got to catch up. This is the '99. We're going backwards."

"Thanks Angelo, but I don't drink wine. I don't like the taste of it and it gives me a headache."

"Who said anything about drinking it? We're tasting it."

Angelo suggested again that he put his beer down and catch up. This seemed more an order now. A polished brass urn being passed around served as a spittoon and Ward became completely confused when he witnessed everyone except Sam expectorating. After rinsing his mouth with a glass of filtered water, Angelo poured him a small dram of the '99 from its decanter and gave him instructions on how to properly taste. The ceremony appeared to Ward a ridiculous waste of time and booze.

"First you hold the balloon by the base and stem. Hold it to the candle light, check out the color for appreciation and memory."

"What's a balloon?"

"The glass; you swirl the wine in a counter clock wise motion then bring it up to your nose and tell me what you sense."

"Why counter clockwise?"

"Because you're right handed."

"I don't smell too much. It doesn't smell like wine though. What's it supposed to smell like?"

"Ward it's not a smell at all. It's a sensation. Sip some as if you're inhaling. Then 'chomp' the wine up and down in your mouth. You should get a few distinct flavors. They don't have to have names at first. Then spit it out, re-rinse and go on to the '98."

The others had been through all three tastings and were now drinking the remainder of each decanter except what Angelo had saved for Ward to sample.

At the upscale restaurant where reservations had been made months in advance by Angelo's secretary, the group settled into a private room and ordered cocktails. Now Ward became utterly confused since there were three empty decanters akin to the ones in the dining room. On the way in the car Ward had to admit that the red wine was better than any wine that he'd ever drunk, not that he'd drunk that much red wine. He confirmed to all that he, his girl friend, his brother, sister, and his parents preferred beer to mixed drinks. Wine had never been a subject for discussion.

"That Chateau Lafite is worth about twelve hundred dollars a bottle now. That's why Sam was the only ass who swallowed the tastings. Angelo would only put up with that from him. He's a drunk. He wasn't about to spit anything out. You'll see tonight."

Sal gave the server three bottles from Angelo's stash while the boss ordered three more very good reds from the wine list. Following the lead, Ward ordered a 'Kettle One' on the rocks. This was a meat crowd this time of year and all brought ravenous appetites to the dinner. The lamb chops, veal chops, and steaks were stacked high on the plates as the wine flowed freely after the initial cocktail. Ward began to accept this new drink as tasty and even refreshing. After a glass at the house he had a glass from each of the three decanted bottles and felt none the worse for it. It couldn't hurt to have more. In fact, he felt nothing at all. Had he had six beers or more he would be lit and would have cut himself off. The hunting trip had already fused a closeness with his bosses and co-workers and they hadn't actually hunted yet. The camaraderie of the wonderful meal with the introduction to 'The Nectar of the Gods', livened the party and the hour had not struck eight. As he sat and enjoyed the atmosphere, bantering and stories, new wine glasses magically appeared in front of him as the wine steward decanted more red wine with professional deftness.

Back at the house by ten, the incessant chatter had given way to utterances of exhaustion and Sam telling himself good night. Ward, not wanting a repeat performance from the morning, changed into the now dry but dank thermal underwear, laid his boots and outer garb in strategic order for dressing then lay atop his still unmussed bed. His thoughts directed themselves toward the good wine and the peaceful, beguiling effect it had upon him. The five A.M.wake up for breakfast would come soon. The drive to Tilghman Island would be brief enough to shove off on the three hired boats and their two men crews by six thirty. With his elongated nap and a full seven hours sleep ahead, Ward fully anticipated his second hunting excursion. As he closed his eyes his last thoughts brought him a new liking for the experience simply of being outdoors for more than ten minutes this time of year. The pale, distant, light of the sunshine, when there was sun, offered still, natural vistas akin to a painting chosen by the artist for that very reason.

He dreamed the dreams of the innocent and transcendent. At an hour somewhere in the night his eyes sprang open. He battled to close them again but lost. Lying fitfully and fully awake he determined the rhythmic breathing of his dorm mates had not been source of his disquiet. Unable to lie comfortably at all, he chose a trip to the bathroom although no urgency demanded it. The moonshine gave the room enough light for Ward to regard his watch. The dial illuminated the hour to be just after one. His head seemed to turn in a direction opposite from his stomach. Carefully closing the door, he opened a cabinet over the sink in search of any over the counter antacid or aspirin. With no luck, he determined that he must slip downstairs since he knew more sleep to be notional at that time. Grabbing his outer gear he slipped quietly down the hall past the other bedrooms. His goal was the comfortable leather couch in the den where he knew an Afghan quilt to be slung over one arm. The vision came to him at first in the form of silhouette, a gigantic shadow formed against the wall at the top of the stairs. As he shuffled backwards to avoid the eerily formed human image, the macabre figure, still only a mirage, spoke to him.

"Didn't I tell you Judy would leave me? She took off with

that carpet installer, I know it."

As the apparition neared, the shadow grew. Ward now backed farther down the same hallway toward his own room.

"Didn't I tell you?"

Ward, clutching his ten articles of clothing, could think of no other solution but to respond.

"No, I didn't know. Who are you?"

"Who am I? Who are you? You're not a carpet installer are you?"

Just then a tall figure emerged from a hall bathroom and made precariously for the top of the staircase. A large head with a lion's mane attached to a flabby corps propped up by spindly legs took short but unmistakable goose steps as if to descend. Dropping everything, Ward rushed to front the somnambulist before it would meet the top riser and be destined for a bigger headache than Ward's; much worse. It was Sam in only his briefs. Only two paces from the top, Ward, with his back to the steps grabbed the banister railing with his left hand and gently placed his right palm on the soft belly of the much larger man.

"So tell me Sam, when exactly did Judy leave?"

His next ploy, if Sam were to make more progress, would be to side step the sleep walker, grab him around the ankles and hope Sam's bulk wouldn't drag them both to the tiled foyer below. The elephantine down coat and pants he'd dropped would make for a nice cushion or even a sled for the stairs but the wide eyed Frankenstein like ogre was planted like a leafy oak between Ward and his mound of goose feathers and polyester.

"When did she leave? When did she leave? She left in nineteen-ninety-two. Rat bastard carpet installer," he hollered.

At that, the younger and stronger man's pressure had been

rewarded as he stood one step down while holding Sam at bay on the landing.

"C'mon Sam, let's get back to bed. I'm sure Judy is still missing you after all these years."

The pair repaired slowly down the hall as Ward guided the man from behind toward the opened door of his bed room and as tenderly as he could push Sam down in a sitting position then slowly leaned the man down on his back.

"Good night Sam. Get some rest."

Sprawled out on the comfortable red leather sofa that reminded him of the color of the wine, he thumbed through a dozen magazines. With no patience for reading to tire his eyes, he chose to toss and turn every two minutes instead of futile attempts to relax. Listening for another episode from Sam precluded any true drowsiness and twice he went up to check on him. Sam slept as sound as Ward wished he could. One multi word mantra did finally console him; 'I'll never drink wine again.' He thought he was asleep and dreaming about the aroma of strong coffee until he heard the slight clamor from the kitchen. It was four thirty and he could barely move and wasn't dreaming but wished he were. As he tried to drift off, even for a half an hour, the whole room burst into a booming shudder which even startled the keepers who were preparing breakfast in the kitchen.

"Up and at 'em my boy. This is a hunting party not a coed sleep over. You were being a little tardy passing that decanter down my end last night. Looks like you've acquired a new vice. I had to switch to rum and coke then to Grand Mariner. Man, you look awful. Looks like you've been up all night. Let me show you how to get some color in those bony cheeks. We'll be the first ones for the fried eggs and oyster fritters soon as they're done. Nice and hot and fried in just a little oil. Man needs his grease after a night like that. You should follow old Sam. Have a few stiff ones after the vino. Makes you sleep like baby. Let's eat before that ravenous crowd gets up."

"No thanks Sam. Let me ask you, how did Angelo come to all this. He drinks expensive French wine, drives German cars and takes the train to New York on weekends to attend the opera. He's the youngest guy in the company and yet he owns it. He's got a home and boat on the Intercoastal in Florida, another home in Cabo. He's the perfect family man, two sons and a third kid on the way. He deals in hundreds of millions every week and he looks like a beach bum," whispering while glancing over his shoulder, Sam acquiesced to Ward's observations.

"His old man is a very rich chap. I've met him. He's a hell of a nice guy. He started out with nothing. Got into real estate at first in southern Missouri where they're from. You know how Missouri borders all those states, well the old man wanted to own property in each state and the rest is history. Angelo came along late in life. His sister is twenty years older. He went to the University of Missouri then became Rhodes Scholar. He wanted to succeed on his own and thought Baltimore had been passed over investment wise. Besides he loves the Bay. He could have just taken over for his father but he wanted the challenge to build a company based on his father's ethics and principles, number one of which is to surround yourself with the most qualified, honest, hard working and loyal people. He can't do it alone."

"Where did the fine arts and wine come from? What's up with his name? Where'd that come from?"

"His mother was an opera singer originally from New Orleans. She sang all over the world. When he was born she said he looked like a little 'angel,' the kind of cherub you see in those old religious paintings. Ward, you look just awful. How'd you sleep last night?"

"Great, how about you Sam?"

"I slept like a bear in winter. Woke up feeling alive and as fresh as the weather. Yeah, Sammy slept great, feels great."

On the way through St. Michael's, Ward had never known to be so hung over before. Every soft turn the vehicle made, hurt. He knew this to be more than the 'morning after the night before' beer bash. Every motion, every sound, every sight introduced him to some new trauma, mental and physical. His only small comfort derived from a new mantra; 'this too will pass' but that was soon replaced with the more prominent, overriding enduring thought; 'God, I wish I weren't here.' He should have never let Sal talk him into the four inch veal chop stuffed with wild shitake mushrooms. 'Yeah, that's the ticket; it's all Sal's fault.' For all the beauty of the of the frigid morning as they approached the bridge to Tilghman Island, he saw only a blurred, jumbled collage of sickening, featureless objects which pained him even to identify; a far cry from yesterday which brought him an alert and novel appreciation of each natural nuance he espied. The boat's engines were running when they arrived and the bubbling hum penetrated his brain like a crane driving a piling deep into the earth. Too proud and embarrassed to beg off, he boarded his assigned craft with Angelo, Sam and Sal. The same theory initiated yesterday prevailed today; 'keep a close eye on Ward and make sure he doesn't harm anyone including himself.'

As the day dawned from the southeast, the three craft armada left the pier from Knapp's Narrows west into the Bay and the wide mouth of the river on whose shores he experienced pensive, reflective musings only a few hours ago and only miles away. According to a map in one of the periodicals he perused while attempting to be carried away in the arms of Morpheus, the distance seemed rather short as the crow flies but they needed to drive a hairpin route to be just down and across the river from the house. When they reached the open Bay, the crews began a series of short, circular voyages as they dropped duck decoys strung together for the purpose of retrieving along with the hopefully abundant venery. At a time when a bright crisp day promised, the sky went grey, a wind blew and the three foot waves began to bob the boat to no certain rhythm. The three real hunters stood steady at their positions on the open stern with good sea legs and held a fixed gaze toward the western sky. For a small diversion Ward went down to the cabin to sit where the taciturn captain and his mate blissfully ignored him. The longest hour of his life took only ten true minutes and whatever discomforts plagued him became a maniacal fate to which he easily resigned and surrendered. Dozing off for few minutes, he was aroused by the mate, "We got ducks."

He knew this was different. He couldn't quite see anything but thought he heard an odd sound neither human nor mechanical. Sam had a wide stance while Sal and Angelo stood with the right foot behind the left. In an instant Sam hollered, "Angelo!"

With that, a spread winged creature came straight up the water for the stern of the boat and Angelo loosed two rounds which only seemed to disable and distract its path. When he went by the port side, Sal brought the luckless fowl down with a single round. Gunfire from the other boats some distance away erupted and illuminated the cold mist with burnt oranges and yellowish reds. By the sound of their barrages more than a single quarry had invaded their air space. Then there was silence. The boat went some thirty yards to fetch the downed prey. Angelo told Ward he'd definitely get his chance to shoot soon. When Ward asked him how he knew as opposed to the day before, he smiled.

"I can smell it," and he meant it.

Instantly a swarm blackened the now drizzly, half dark sky and flew upon them. Ward watched as the expert shots brought down whatever they aimed at. A brief lull allowed the captain to circle a hundred yard radius while the mate fished the fallen game from the choppy, icy waves with a long pole with a hook attached. For no known reason, Ward was surprised that the ducks floated. The mate deposited them in a wooden locker built hard against the stern which on less bloody excursions could serve as seats. Angelo asked Ward to load his new weapon as he had been instructed but to keep the gun broken open until Angelo and only he directed the newcomer to action. Now the firing from eleven shooters and twenty-two barrels echoed violently into a foreboding heaven and when most triggers fired their arms simultaneously, the deafening roar could be confused for cannon fire. Ward didn't know how much longer the sport would last but it had been less than an hour since all the decoys had been set. The full boxes of shells for each man didn't seem to be depleted and each new squadron of fowl seemed to be larger than the last. Now his feet felt the icy weather through his boots, his face a frozen mask in spite of a high temperature that rendered him feverish. When the wooden locker seemed full, he wished the end of the morning to be near. Only when the mate stored more felled feathers and flesh in two unused gang boxes did he fall martyr to his own dyspeptic nausea. As the sturdy wooden craft heaved, dropped and rose more dramatically his maladies obliged him to abandon courage for the resignation of self pity.

"What do they do with all these ducks?" he asked the mate straining to make his voice audible.

"They donate them to the local needy people who pluck 'em, skin 'em and eat 'em. Problem is they got to be careful because all that shot that's in 'em. Biting down on one of those pellets can break their teeth and it's tough to get to get it all out. Besides these ducks have tough meat. These birds need to be culled anyway so it's not as bad as it looks."

Just then Angelo alerted Ward to come aft. Standing beside him, he listened as attentively as he could while Sam and Sal reloaded on the port side. Ward's abandoned starboard side faced the island to the east and he had seen no quarry come from that direction. As he awaited the next incoming wave of ducks he noticed the top of the full locker smeared in blood. A crop appeared coming from the southwest; he prepared himself as best he could to shoot down one of these undaunted strong winged creatures. With only little concentration, his imminent chore delivered him momentarily from morbid illness as he attended to the mental preparation of his baptism.

"Fire at the one I tell you to. Squeeze nice and steady. One barrel then the second. Relax and take a deep breath, in through the nose, out through the mouth. Ready, Ward?"

"I really think I am. After all, this is why you all brought me."

'What a lie,' he thought.

As the densest flock yet approached with some alacrity directly up the Bay toward the stern, Angelo nodded and Ward closed his gun and sighed more than breathed. Following directions he drew the artistically made weapon to his shoulder for sighting and kept his eyes peeled for an area that might produce his assigned target from Angelo. In his brain he felt stillness, even a hush as he readied to take direct aim and fire; silence. He heard the woeful screech before he became aware of its origin. The hood of the locker sprang open almost catching him under the chin. A prehistoric aberration leaped vertically within an inch of Ward's forehead and for the briefest moment their eyes locked upon each other as his nose and the bleeding duck's beak contacted each other akin to an Eskimo kiss. Ward didn't think he could feel anything except the sickness of his mind and body but he was wrong. The fowl dropped back down into its hold and before he could act or react, the same wounded escapee rebounded with the same violent upward attempt at freedom. This episode provided a deeper and longer penetration of their eyes as a broad flapping wingspan made a more distinct impression of prehistory. Ward could feel the cool forced air from the duck's persistence at heavier than air flight. His difficulty at becoming air borne made it that much more impossible because of his mortal wounds. A third feeble attempt failed as Angelo seized the interloper and wrung his neck then slammed the carcass back into its coffin. As Angelo rearmed and told Ward to follow his lead, a curious sensation overcame him that he'd felt since Sam had mentioned fried eggs at four thirty that morning. While the mate had retreated abaft to aid in any more strangulation, he caught a glimpse of Ward and knew. In a daze of confusion he could see Angelo handing him his gun, could see that he was talking to him but there was no comprehension. As

Angelo neared to repeat whatever he'd been shouting, the full throttle of Ward's sick took dead aim. The stream of red wine discolored by stomach enzymes had the radius and force of a typical fire hose at a three alarm fire. The first volley struck Angelo dead in the chest and forced him backward a step. It couldn't be told whether the barrage or the horror had moved him.

"We've got a 'chummer!'" the mate close by heralded.

A second even more forceful burst caught his boss clearly under the chin. Sam and Sal stood staring and immobilized as if the violent projectile vomiting had supplanted hunting as the day's sport. If anything, Ward couldn't budge and it was up to Angelo, who was attempting to turn Ward and bend him over the stern of the boat, to dodge the third heaving stream of sick. This volley was violently hurled with the chunks of veal and shrapnel pieces of shitakes. The eruption proved to be the most satisfying puke since it missed its previous victim and began to relieve Ward of what ailed him. The last two blows shot harmlessly over the back and into the water. Ward's cleansing brought him a renaissance and speedily rehabilitated his body and mind. Left alone he remarked on his future which, at best, seemed perilous.

"The fish will eat today. Thanks, Chum," the mate hollered laughingly.

The following weekend Ward returned to Cambridge. He spent two lightly snowy days looking at small properties and homes close to or on the Choptank. He would have stayed over on Monday but feared the weather. Angelo held meetings on Monday mornings and he never liked to be late.

❖ ❖ ❖ ⛵ ❖ ❖ ❖

A Day on The Bay

There's something to be said about not being on the job while the rest of the work-a-day world toils for their masters. The small company's employees gathered together for a day of recreation on a 'Blue Tuesday.' Now any time of the week would suffice for a day off sponsored by the firm and its owner, even if it were spent with co-workers but by passing Tuesdays gave the group that special sensation of getting something over on the rest of the nation back to the grind after a beautiful weekend. The work week would begin on Wednesday and therefore accelerate faster to Friday because of the 40 percent head start. The rented luxury bus brought the forty employees from their offices near Baltimore, hard by the Middle River, to the Annapolis city pier on Dock Street where the modern motor yacht waited to cruise the excited group across the Bay to St. Michaels for lunch at 'The Crab Claw.' For all the fine crab houses in and around Baltimore, every employee had visited the St. Michaels' landmark more than once but only by car. The perfect, deep harbor on the Miles River held a genuine fascination for all visitors especially local Marylanders and Virginians because of its American history, unique shopping and appealing quaintness. Like so many places in coves, creeks and rivers just off the Bay, St. Michaels maintained its character despite its popularity. So easily accessible from route fifty or from so many marinas it centered in mid Bay, the town led by good example to its neighboring small port towns and shared the pride in their successes. The Bay now boasted at least a hundred smaller like towns and villages along its shores. They had restored and maintained as much of their original character as could be saved. Each professed its own history with refurbished artifacts, implements and water craft from a bygone era not only to show visitors but as gentle reminder to themselves of a heritage worthy of remembrance. By honoring the fruitful life that the Bay had provided to generations, the inhabitant's love committed a promise to regenerate, revive and respect the water of today and tomorrow. The Chesapeake Bay Maritime Museum next to the restaurant with its exhibits and grounds was always worthy of a visit.

Because the modern motor coach arrived a little early, Thomas, Danny and Troy made a short promenade up to Main Street, around the circle and because they had time, walked up the street leading up to the state house and away from the water. They needed to walk off the sumptuous, gourmet catered breakfast the company served very early in the office cafeteria before embarking down Interstate 97. The city shined in the warm September sun and warmed them as they trod up West Street. They remarked the illuminated dome of the historic capitol as it glistened like a beacon. The three co-workers had become friends since beginning with the small but dynamic technology firm two years ago. Only Troy was a native Baltimorean as were about ten of the firm's employees. The others arrived from different states and backgrounds. One common thread, however, was woven through the employee persona vitae, security clearances. Even the janitors, called 'maintenance', were full time workers for the company, and not an outside firm, also had clearances. They were on the trip as well. No one was above or below the requirement and each was vetted bi-annually. Not by design but by the nature of their work, most were between their late twenties and mid thirties. Certain amounts of experience learned with previous employers, for example the military, were requisite. Not everyone had or needed a college degree. Danny, a Navy vet and a project leader of many engineering and math grads had barely survived high school yet he bore out the owner's dictum; education does not mean intelligence or ability. The man thought it the exception these days when a job candidate possessed all three.

As the three made their way back to the dock for the departure, the city seemed to be all theirs. The midshipmen must all be in class or not required to be there yet, no one knew. For sure the General Assembly was not in session. All the tourists had disappeared and it was too early in the school year to have the city hosting field trips. Embarkation hinted at a luxury cruise and the firm's owner stocked the air conditioned gathering room below, like one finds on a larger cruise. The man started his company after working in the same industry in its formative years, decades earlier. He not only believed he should treat his workers with respect and dignity, he lived it. Being the owner meant that he worked as hard for his people as they did for him.

'Family', outside its true definition had become an over used cognate for close personal relationships on sports teams and businesses but his paternal care for these good people manifested itself daily. When adding a new hire, he looked for quality of individual character strength as much as their skills to perform the work. An applicant needed to excel in both to secure a position.

Re-greeting his employees individually as they boarded, Dr. Brandt, their paternal benefactor wished them a great day and thanked each one for all their hard work. They in turn thanked him. The young captain and his crew shoved off at the bottom of 'Ego Alley.' He backed her out of the berth and kept the mid sized pleasure ship at four knots until drifting right into the channel, past Eastport and into the still Bay. Picking up some speed as she steadied on a course south-southeast, the day trippers looked up at the Bay Bridge and a tanker anchored just off the port bow. The passengers mostly found themselves on both decks, the smaller open cabin being topside. At an indeterminate speed they picked just enough pace so that the breeze refreshed without whipping caps and visors off and slow enough that the diesel engines didn't inhibit conversations at the rail. Part of the group plan required Danny and Margie, his top team lieutenant, to monitor communications from the office. Although a general message at the main switchboard and each employee's extension told of the company's closure that day, an emergency could announce itself at any time, day or night. The unique business of the firm was to check, verify and certify detailed technical and scientific work that the federal government had contracted out. The firm guaranteed the produced results of the work to be accurate. Most was done for the Department of Defense. In the recent past, as well as for decades many private firms had often overcharged the tax payer while delivering an inefficient bloated almost useless product over due and over budget. At the instigation of a Maryland congresswoman 'contract work checkers' were developed to alleviate government agencies from dealing with the plethora of these issues.

In Mid Bay the captain called Dr. Brandt to the bridge. The crew member told him of the request with some urgency. Almost instantaneously cell phones began to ring, chime and vibrate. As soon as the calls were answered they disappeared and 'call failed' messages lit up the screens on every phone as soon as a return call was attempted. Except for Danny none could get through. He wore two phones, a regular cell phone and an advanced military version capable of functions which would remain unknown to the general public for several years. Normal service had been either shut off by the provider or they were too far removed from the closest towers and being at sea level. Dr. Brandt called a meeting of the entire group in the larger conference and party room on the main deck.

"The captain has just told me that one of the World Trade Centers in New York has been hit by an airplane. At this point we don't know what the story is. It sounds like a terrible accident. Before we could get any more information or clarification, his ship to shore transmission terminated and he believes not on his end. Has anyone received any calls?"

"We all have but there's no service," proclaimed a voice from the back which became accompanied by a chorus of agreement.

"Until we find out, we're proceeding to St. Michaels. We've reached the center point of the Bay so we're a little closer to the eastern shore than back to Annapolis. It's the captain's call. He's the boss. We may drop anchor in Eastern Bay and not make it to the restaurant but he's going to see what's up. I know you all want to go back but this is the most prudent thing for now."

At that point Danny came in with an ashened face which had all his summer tan flushed from it. He had just spoken to his French wife at home with their four month old daughter in Timonium.

"I've got Bridgette on the code 'e' defense line. The other tower building has just been hit. They showed it on television. Nobody seems to know what's going on and if they do, they're not saying anything. I've asked her to call me back when the TV people up date the situation. New York city is in a general panic."

"Does anybody's cell work out here? This thing has an imperfect charge tolerance and I didn't want to run the battery down."

Everyone attempted again to call out with no good results. With a common groan but no panic, all eyes were focused on Danny and Brandt. The captain had slowed the progress of the ship to a more maneuverable speed to preserve fuel and to alter his destination if need be.

"We'll tie up in about an hour in St Michaels. Danny, try her again."

He dialed and began to listen with his left index finger in the same sided ear. Nothing could be discerned by his expression, demeanor or body language. The give away was Danny's waving his co-workers close to him.

"The first tower that was hit has been completely destroyed. It showed a wave of fire, rescue and police reinforcements entering the building five minutes before it collapsed. This is an attack. The other building is billowing smoke but still standing.

My parents are on the way over to my place. Bridgette is too upset to give clear details. She's only been speaking English for four years. She's watching on TV and I can't get all she's saying. I just know that it's terrible and she's extremely upset. Our cell service should get better the closer we get to shore. Wait, it's my father."

After a seemingly interminable silence, he closed the phone.

"The Pentagon has been attacked. He thinks it must have been about the same time as the Trade centers."

The firm worked with and for the Armed Forces. Everyone knew some workers there. Dr. Brandt, a retired Air Force Colonel and PhD in electrical engineering, knew the most.

After some brief speculations, a quiet ensued to everyone's comfort. The notions previously bandied around briefly did not serve the situation well. As Dr. Brandt returned to the bridge, the entire ensemble gathered out on deck for much needed fresh air and soulful reflection. The hum of the engines broke no one's pensive mood. Now the captain had opened the throttle challenging them to deliver his ship to a safe harbor. A distinct feeling of true closeness embraced the group, closeness deeper than the already tight-knit clan thought possible. The solace grew from the common situation, one of uncertainty, helplessness and inability to communicate combined with everyone's fear and trepidation about their own families who now seemed much farther away than just up the Bay.

The first sign of concern came as the southern sky, full of cloudless sun all morning, began to alter dead ahead as the bow aimed. With an embroidered tinge of some indeterminate shade, the specks grew larger as the motor yacht approached the darkened image; or was the now gray-blue spider like aberrations nearing them? The captain's voice, without distress, directed all passengers inside to the larger deck cabin. A few lingered on deck as the diesel engines were drowned out by the coming thunderous roars. The overhead sunlight shone like a klieg lamp on the top of the two Air Force F15s as they jetted toward them. At no more than one hundred yards above sea level, the attack fighters, one to the starboard, the other port side, roared up to the ship near enough for the pilots to observe her markings. Close enough indeed, for the recalcitrant few who remained at the railing to see the four flyers, the two pilots and two weapon's officers look down at them in the briefest instant. Even from their distinctive bubble cock pits through their masks, they could see the Danny and Troy eyeballing them back in return. Another call for all passengers to go and remain inside, this time with distinct urgency, found the crew readying life vests for each passenger and attempting to instruct the passengers at uncertain procedures which were mute because of pulsating crescendo of the fighters.

As soon as the two war planes, which were carrying sophisticated ordinance under their fuselages according to Dr. Brandt, screamed just past the boat, the pilots pulled their sticks, nosed skyward, accelerated with violent bursts of force and ascended almost vertically. From the fantail Danny and Dr. Brandt witnessed the rear of the fiery exhausts of the jet engines almost overhead as they roared skyward. Retreating hastily back inside, the two men of science knew all too well the physics of the impending reaction of the planes' forced air intake and the absolute certain consequences of the exhaust propulsion and the discordant, unbearable roar of the speeding jet engines' vibrating impact on the water below. The tumultuous speed of the fighters concussed the ship and Bay violently. With a knowing look of instant agreement, both men motioned all their co-workers on the floor inside as they moved quickly among them and pushing down all those whose terror had rendered them motionless. At first it appeared as if four giant holes had been excavated in the Bay for the purpose of driving pylons the size and shape of a silo. The displacement and depth created vacuums which may have never been seen on the Bay before; especially considering the heavy density of its salt water. Even then the water remained calm for a second save for the pronounced wake of the vessel now at a speed which almost imperiled her ability to remain intact. So shakily did the ship rattle and creek sideways from her own speed and the plane's velocity, that it felt as if she may break apart in any direction except backwards.

When the phenomena began to replace air with water, the craters seemed to fill themselves up with as much natural dynamic force as the unnatural propulsion and concussion of the jets which had caused them. Now from behind, in spite of the maximum knot speed demanded by the ship's pilot, oceanic waves rose and hurtled themselves toward the craft as she desperately attempted in vain to outpace the cascading tumult of the tidal force. Although the skipper of the recreational chartered yacht was the youngest member of the crew, even the youngest skipper in the company, his remarkable skills in seamanship on the water and brilliance in the classroom had made his promotion from deck hand to captain a certainty. Yet, no one could be ill or well prepared for this dire emergency. Of course all who sail the Bay have been caught in some violent weather, dense fogs and sundry potential mishaps. This was different. The captain, Brandt and Danny knew that the vessel may be ill prepared to accommodate and survive the rush of man made tidal waves about to crash down upon them.

The violent thunder of the jet engines had abated only to be replaced by the cacophony of the pounding of the overly stressed engines below and the threatening clamor of the first crash of mountain high water abaft. What certainly forged a blessing and curse simultaneously, came from the distance which the ship tried to put between itself and the eminent blow of the first wave and the exaggerated wake rising high above the second deck. The rumbling tidal waves had forced the ship's wake forward instead of aside and aft. The forced redirection of wake and a heaving vortex of salt water pounded the ship not built for such a circumstance. Lying flat on the deck of the large entertainment cabin, hearts pounded at pace with the rumbling engines below. The ship heaved and shuddered like a toy boat at the bottom of a mountain waterfall. Wave after wave, seemingly simultaneously, battered the ship and the first sixty seconds of the assault lasted an hour in the minds of the terrified passengers. No sound could be heard from drowned out screams, entreaties and prayers, only animated, horrifying facial expressions told of the terror. When the small liner began to right itself, the rolling surf still made standing impossible. After a fashion, the crew crawled from group to group to check and help with injuries. By the time they were able to look up, the forsaken sun streamed through the cabin's splashed windows as if to calm and soothe. A flurry of commiseration among people found themselves in tight embraces and thankful tears. The gift of cell phone communication restored itself as they entered the Eastern Bay and neared landfall possessing satellite towers.

Forgotten for no small amount of time were the earlier catastrophic events to which they had been not been totally privy.

Shaken but sound, they disembarked at the restaurant's dock and strode slowly to the entrance. Only a few injuries were suffered, a crewman's sprained ankle and various other bruises and nicks all tended to with care by the crew. Inside they found a few diners gathered around the bar staring incredulously at the televisions. Immobile from their incident, aghast at the news and heartbroken for the victims, the rattled group found no appetite but camaraderie with the few mid afternoon lunch patrons who couldn't leave the minute by minute breaking news. The restaurant staff, also just as shaken, helped admirably by answering questions as best they could about any earlier televised reports and details and served the group well with refreshments.

As Dr. Brandt, Danny, Troy and Thomas wandered down the steps outside and toward the pier where the watermen had brought the crabs in earlier that day for the group, the three young men wondered aloud to their boss about the events and actions of the fighter pilots.

"Doctor, I don't get it, do you? I can't believe those guys wouldn't know what effect they'd have on us out there in the middle of the Bay. I don't want to think that they were hot-rodding no matter what the situation."

"Yeah, what do you think they were doing and where were they going?"

"Were they out there on some mission?"

Before the man answered the three, he paused and thought.

"Guys, I may have a feel for what they were doing but I'm not completely sure."

"How do you mean?"

"After the events of this morning which are continuing and the little we know now, the chances are that the military would have scrambled a defensive umbrella over Washington, major strategic installations and had the FAA call down and ground any and all planes in the air, private and especially commercial. No American air space was to be occupied except by military aircraft. It'll probably stay that way for some time."

"So that's what the Air Force guys were doing?"

"They must have come up from Langley Air Force Base in Norfolk, straight up the Bay. We all noticed that there were no boats on the water this morning. It's Tuesday. Not even a wisp of a breeze was up so no sailboats were out. All the power boaters were back to work like everyone else. We must have seemed an anomaly just cruising along, so they thought they'd take a look at us on their way. They were not at mach speed thankfully. I don't know what would have happened if we had borne the brunt of their 'ABs.'"

"On their way where, where were they headed? What are 'ABs?'"

"After Burners. They were deployed to the Academy. That's where they are now. They're part of the defensive perimeter for a place which sends its graduates to stand against and fight the terrorists who attacked us today. I think they knew when they shot past us their speed and exhaust would give us trouble. Their coordinates probably told them to climb just where we were. I think they used some savvy. Since they were going to check out that tanker anchored out in the Bay south of the Bridge, they gave us a look too. They probably calculated that they were past us enough to climb but we know it was awful close. I watched them. One kept north and banked west, the other one turned due west. Then they'll join the air protection coverage over and around Washington. That way at several hundred feet apart they could maximize the protection with proper spacing flying toward each other."

"What were their orders if they encountered a commercial airliner?"

"They'd radio it to land and wonder why the plane hadn't heeded air traffic control orders to get down already. They'd lead it down if necessary. If that failed they'd make quick visual contact with the airlines' cockpit and use the international sign language to get out of the sky and land."

"What happens if the airline doesn't respond? What if it's hijacked, Doctor?"

"Not just hijacked, intending to crash kamikaze-like into a symbolic target and cause the greatest number of casualties, not unlike the events of an hour ago. They'll have a tanker refueling them soon. N.O.R.A.D. will have A.W.A.C.s in the air as well."

"Dr. Brandt, would they really shoot down an airliner full of American lives, one of our own with innocent men, women and children on board to prevent that from happening? Can that possibly be? Is that why they're up there now? How could an American pilot do that?"

"When I would meet a group of pilots, I could tell who the jumbo cargo guys were, who piloted the Air Force Ones and who flew the first line F15s. They all had wings but you could tell them by their personalities. Those fighter guys all have a common look and demeanor. They're special in an eerie way. It's almost scary. It didn't matter if they had baby faces. It was in their eyes."

"So what you're saying is that they would follow orders and shoot down our own people maybe, even as we speak."

"Yes."

❖ ❖ ❖ ⚓ ❖ ❖ ❖

Easton Summertime

Seasons come and seasons go. Some are marked by traditional weather which can be felt by the altered air temperature. Some can be seen by the effect those climate changes have on the nature around us. Some man made seasons are indeterminable. Football 'season' begins in August (with colleges anyway, for now), while baseball 'season' can end closer to Thanksgiving than Labor Day. In the minds of most, summer begins on Memorial Day weekend, runs through the Fourth of July and ends on Labor Day. The migration of birds follows no Julian calendar nor do animals that awake from hibernation on exactly the correct day. No matter where one lives, prune the roses when the forsythia blooms.

So it is that each May the 'Blue Ghost' sails up the Bay to the Choptank, that most noble and widest of Eastern Shore rivers. She turns easily into the Tred Avon, past the plying Oxford-Belleview Ferry with a wave then up to Easton's minimal waterfront. Since the Easton Point Marina was too shallow for the 'Ghost's' draught she tied up next door up at the 'Boathouse' marina at the North neck on Port Street at the edge of town. A special parallel slip is reserved for her each summer. Many days found her in the river anchored outside the channel. The tall yacht never seemed to arrive on the same day and some seasons not even the same week. A few years ago the locals at the Easton Point Marina missed her until mid June. The state of the Blue Ghosts' sails was in disrepair. The masts and rigging seemed to beg for straightening. When local sailors at the marina inquired after her skipper about the tardiness of his arrival, his terse reply only deepened the mystery surrounding him.

"Boys, it's not like a scheduled train out there."

Where 'out there' was no one knew exactly, only that it included what the French call 'au large', on the open sea. The solo sailor had become a notorious summertime topic of conversation in local bars and restaurants. From clap board shanty beer joints to comfortable club rooms with plush leather arm chairs, almost everyone in Easton, indeed the nearby towns of St. Michaels and Cambridge, had heard and repeated stories and reports of this intrepid mariner. People who had never seen him or the sleek fifty and a half foot, navy blue- hulled sailing yacht he called home, passed around third hand rumors as if they were intimately connected to him. After the first ten summers of suddenly appearing in spring like an apparition then vanishing like a mirage in early September, the sloop's christened name only deepened the captain's enigma.

His routine varied little. Some mornings would find him gone but his locked gang box told of an imminent return, usually by late evening. About twice a summer the 'Blue Ghost' would live up to her moniker and disappear for a couple of days only to be serenely anchored two mornings later almost mid river. On those late night returns, open water was chosen to avoid the clamor of tying up at the slip. The captain actually preferred the privacy of the beautiful unbusy river. The pilot of the single manned crew bore a distinct resemblance to a great American writer of the last century. This 'Hemingwayesque' figure earned or inherited the nickname, 'Papa' among the more literate tavern dwellers. So those who came to refer to him by this gentle reference may or may not have known of the origin of this sobriquet, yet used it familiarly. The uncanny resemblance was not that of the old Ernest Hemingway, a depressed recluse who was a suicide victim. This 'Papa' was of the sandy bearded, barrel- chested adventurer who ran with the bulls in Spain, taunted a U-Boat while fishing off the Keys during the war, accompanied the 'Free French' forward army units in the liberation of Paris and made it with Ava Gardner in Africa.

On fine mornings he could be found sitting on the polished teak deck facing the rising sun and computer screen of a rather expensive looking lap top. A steaming cup of tea poured from a unique oriental porcelain pot accompanied him above deck afterwards as he moved from one small maintenance chore to another. After emerging from below at mid morning, Papa brought up a finely made twelve speed bicycle attached the front wheel, walked to the street then went about what could definitely be referred to as his daily constitutional of exercise. Wearing a too small helmet made him a small figure of fun to the children he'd encounter on their bikes on Port Street. His warm smile, at least to anyone under fourteen, disarmed the kids and they greeted him with calls of "Hi Papa." Even the vacationed school children had heard and learned the lore of the yachtsman who called Easton 'home' three months a year in summertime. In their case however, they had actually seen him in person and exchanged rudimentary yet real dialogue with the man.

On his return after working up a good sweat, if he didn't shove off for some excursion which he fancied, Papa planned to be in town for the day. After a shower below, he would towel off on deck in swim trunks and could be heard to roar like a Grizzly as he shook the remaining filtered water from his hair and beard. Coming topside in tan Bermuda shorts and Hawaiian shirt, he seemed the epitome of the well-to-do yachtsman. Waiting until past noon, he bicycled different streets to admire the architecturally beautiful town yet usually found himself at the 'News Center Bookshop' perusing the shelves and chatting amicably with the proprietors about out of print best sellers, great literature and dynamic non-fiction. His eclectic tastes in these genres could hardly identify any personality traits to his character. After buying a thoughtful selection and placing an order for some out of print tome, he rode down the street to Mason's to lunch on their fresh catch of the day while he perused the recent purchase. Usually the meal accompanied two glasses of their better Chardonnay or if the mood struck, a bottle of white, usually the Grgich Hills Reserve, from the very good wine list. Still only having two glasses with lunch, he'd cork the remainder and send it back with the server to enjoy with the kitchen after work later that night. Not counting his generous gratuities, these thoughtful offers of sharing rendered him a hushed popularity and praise from the staff which only deepened the riddle of the man. Few patrons did that.

Hopefully seated at the two-top at the closed end of the

front porch in order to have only one table as a neighbor, he appeared content in his solitude but also enjoying the stream of lively chatter from his co-patrons and the animated strollers as they passed by. As often as he could, he attended the Chamber Music Festival performed every June and rarely missed a performance. If this were as close as he could come to enjoying the rewards of a 'boulevardier' without being in some humid, dusty metropolis, he happily accepted. By the end of the night, the day's purchase would have been read and stacked in a pile of like books to be donated to local libraries, hospitals and charities usually in town. He loved Easton which he believed to possess an outlet for every passion he held dear. Papa could never sail with the number of books he accumulated in his travels. Although the below deck quarters and galley were spacious, he detested clutter. If any thing, he preferred any extra space to tempt him to expand the fully stocked, refrigerated wine cabinets. The beer cooler filled with Pacifio, Corona, Tecate, and Red Stripe more than indicated his taste for imported lagers and ales. It also read as a map of his travels since no American domestic tax had been stamped or paid on any case; the beer was purchased from the country that produced it.

The paneled library shelves of the main cabin included many classics including Shakespeare, Dickens, Hardy, Orwell, etc. and, three from the real 'Papa', the autobiographical *A Moveable Feast*, *The Sun Also Rises* and *The Old Man and The Sea*. Jack London, Robert Louis Stevenson, Herman Melville and Joseph Conrad held the distinction of having the most and well thumbed and dog eared pages. Even the worn manner of the page corners of these nineteenth century ocean adventure authors told no real clue about the complexity of the man. They were turned by a left thumb meaning to most that the owner-reader to be left handed. This assumption would be correct had they seen him as a south paw first baseman in college, throw championship darts as a lefty and skeet shoot from the 'wrong' shoulder; incorrect had they seen him relief pitch, bowl cricket and sign his name right handed. Papa played tennis left, golf right. His athletic, agile gait necessitated the ability for solo crossings of oceans. Good sea legs rivaled the importance of a good compass. The meaning of 'ambidextrous' had never known a better definition than him.

On evenings when no occasion marked his well kept calendar, kept in his own hand next to the log, the lone diner of countless meals would happily create dinner mentally. With much verve he donned his chef's apron in the state of the art galley. After his three o'clock yoga session below deck, he jauntily rode to the markets in town looking for the freshest vegetables available. It mattered little to him what they were, though he would never pair two starches or have all greens. Late in June the garlic would be just pulled from the rich soil of the Eastern Shore and in late July and early August the heavenly tomatoes would eat like the delicious fruit they are. If he were to dine in on Saturdays when the farmers' markets opened, Papa would greet the vendors early morning as they arrived and helped some older growers un-load and set up. They had become well acquainted with each other and the early hour gave them both some time to commiserate about the 'going-ons' with their land and his sea. As a last stop he would pick up the two pounds of fresh jumbo lump he had ordered the morning before. Once a summer he would invite acquaintances, husband and wife, who shared his love of the sea, sail and Easton and they would reciprocate with steamed crabs on the deck of their beautiful home on the river. They had been coming to Easton for forty summers from Towson, since their children were young. Grandly situated in a picturesque cove, the magnificent property would be well beyond their means at today's prices. Their own thirty-eight foot boat had been given to their son and daughter-in-law who, for practical purposes now, docked it on the James River in Hopewell, Virginia and nearer their home. The couple in their mid seventies had replaced their old 'third home' with a more manageable, smaller sloop on which to drift down the river and on nice days to Oxford for the great crab cakes at the Robert Morris Inn. The dinners began a few years after they had nodded the sailor's the tacit 'ahoy' to one another as they met in Oxford on occasion or passed on the water. It was years before they actually spoke and it was Papa who initiated it after he noticed some abnormality needing attention with the couple's storm jib.

He liked them not only for their quiet decency and devotion to sailing but for the wide berth they gave him in the early years. No forced interrupting inquiries about his name, where he was from or other prying, disquieting chatter as was the wont of so many well meaning souls who seemed mesmerized by this arcane, solitary figure. The good neighbors knew of the quiet type of self-reliant sailor who eschewed garrulous, discursive small talk for the comforting sounds of wind straining canvases; thus they treated him early on.

He prepared the same dish each year for them as he had the first, something akin to a tradition. Thick beautiful Grouper he'd bought at sea that winter from Cuban fishermen on perilous boats well inside that country's territorial waters served as the main course. After skinning and filleting them in February, he wrapped and froze them on board. Starting with the chef's own creation of chilled white asparagus crab salad, he sliced zucchini, carrot curls, diced pimento and added pepper, mustard and tarragon; not to mention three sliced spears and a third of a pound crab in each. The salad tempted the palate without sating the appetite. Broiled in white wine, fresh lemon, pepper and saltless butter he smothered the filets with another pound of crab meat after sautéing the almost egg size lumps delicately to warm only in lightest amount of olive oil with a slight touch of JO spice. The creation welled up all the savory flavors of the Gulf of Mexico and The Chesapeake Bay without one diminishing or overriding the other. Boiled new potatoes sliced open and stuffed with butter and roasted garlic and finely rinsed steamed, fresh kale completed the entrée. With the hors d' oeuvre of Beluga caviar he poured the subtly crisp Pinot Blanc from Demetria. He accompanied the salad with a Pinot Noir from Clos Pepe in the cool Santa Rita Hills. For dinner he offered a favorite red, La Croce, half Syrah, half Sangiovese, from Stolpman. He had picked up these little gems in Santa Barbara on a sail on his twin brother's ninety foot sailing yacht from Monterey to Cabo San Lucas the previous autumn. Only the unwashed foodies would object to red wine with fish but this combination of dominating seafood and the well crafted, light and sensitive wines melded the two serenely. It takes an adventurous host and chef not to pair bold distinctive dishes with dominant, big alcohol wines. To succeed at the reverse justified the challenge.

As Papa knew the situation would present itself, the morning arrived Labor Day weekend when the two men in dark suits and darker glasses stopped on the dock at the bow of the 'Blue Ghost' turned down her pier and stood parallel to amidships and made a cursory inspection of their surroundings. They were pros and it stood out a mile to the trained eye. Certainly the two were professionals in their trade yet not old and therefore experienced sufficiently enough in matters not taught them in their rigorous training.

"Hello in there, is anybody home?"

"Maybe he's jumped over to another boat."

"No, he's here. We saw him go down stairs thirty minutes ago and he hasn't come out yet."

After pacing the length of the yacht with suit coats opened, Papa smilingly addressed them from the stern under the matching blue sunbrella and they had no idea how he got there without them noticing him.

"Good morning. May I help you young men?"

Already slightly dismayed by his sudden presence, they were put at slight disadvantage by him referencing their youth and maybe experience at least compared to his.

"Mr. Attenbourgh, I'm federal agent Johnson and this is agent Harlow. We're with the U.S. Treasury. We'd like to come over on your boat to speak with you."

"I know where you are from. Permission to board is denied."

"Pardon me, sir did you say we can't come on the boat?"

"No, I said, Permission to board is denied."

"Isn't that the same thing?"

"Yes, I guess it is in a way but you asked me what I said and I repeated it."

"Why won't you let us come over? You're not hiding any thing are you?"

"I have everything to hide from you two and any other strangers who ask to come aboard."

"Wait a minute, Johnson. Sir, why can't we come on your boat? We've shown you our badges and photo identifications. If you don't speak with us we'll find another way."

"I didn't say I wouldn't speak with you. You're just not welcome on my boat."

"Why is that?"

"Firstly, you're armed. Secondly, you have leather shoes on and thirdly, you're both wearing neckties. Now, under International Maritime laws of which The United States of America is a signatory, a captain can refuse any uninvited persons, especially armed, from boarding his vessel. It goes back to our Barbary Coast days with pirates and before that English law. The other two rules are mine."

"Well, we'll ask our questions out here for anyone within earshot to hear. It could be something you might not want people to eavesdrop since you have everything to hide. Otherwise we can get pretty insistent with you if we want, no good cop bad cop, just two bad cops."

"I know most of these folks around here and as you can see most boats are out on the water. They've known me or of me for a long time around here. Besides it doesn't matter to me if they hear what you say, only what I might."

"You are on a dinner guest list tomorrow evening at a home here in Talbot County at which highly placed government officials may be present. You've already 'R.S.V.P.'d. You know we have to investigate any and all invitees especially if they haven't been vetted by the Secret Service in quite some time. Also in asking around town, we've heard that you're a bit of an eccentric. We just thought we'd come by and check you out. That's all. So look 'F. Scott' or whatever your literary alias is, you tell us what we want to know and we don't mess with you for the next twelve hours."

"Mr. Harlow, that's not all at all. You've known that I was on the list over a week ago. You've pulled everything on me you can get your hands on. Your people have court ordered warrants to hack my computer. They ran every conceivable secret code busting device they have to read my emails going back years. They perused every web site I've pulled lately. They checked every port of call I've made in the last ten years by screening my passport declarations, foreign entries and re-entries all in the name of national security. How did you know my name was Attenbourgh if you haven't seen volumes of photos of me? I could have been a workman, a crew member, a thief. No, you knew who I was by recognition. You've been scanning every newspaper clipping, magazine article, on me back when I was skinny. You've done a, no, at least two psychological analysis this week on me by two separate profilers, probably one of yours from the 'bureau' and one from the 'company.' That lot you work for are pathetic, autocratic paranoids. You haven't gotten reports from locals about my weird behavior. I get on swell here. The people are wonderful. This has been my home every summer for over ten years. My family used to have a home here. My father brought me from New York when I was a kid to sail and fish and crab. There was a lot of money here then, still is. The locals used to call us the 'station wagon set.' I may not be the most open guy but I'm not running for mayor either. As for your 'high ranking government officials', you are referring to the Secretary of State, Chairman of the Federal Reserve and the Vice President."

Just then a deck phone rang and as Papa went to pick it up

in its box to answer, the two agents separated from each other by ten feet, assumed a wide stance and initiated a defensive posture while at the ready. Harlow spoke, "Slowly."

Papa answered the line without haste hoping his little tête-à-tête with these boys hadn't riled them too awfully.

"Hello. Yes, this is he. Yes, I can hold. Yes, hello, hello. I've been well. I read that your health improves. I'm happy for it. I didn't expect you to respond by phone. You're a busy guy. Yes, I look forward to it as well. It's been a along time. Yes they are charming fellows in an 'Abilene' sort of way. Well, if you think that's best, hold on. See you Saturday. It's for you."

Stretching the line to the pier, he handed the receiver to Johnson who was closest. As soon as the agent heard the first syllable on the other line, he cupped the receiver and whispered to Harlow.

"It's 'Cowhand,' it's the Vice President!"

"Christ Johnson, are you messing with me?"

"No, here."

"Hello, yes sir, thank you for staying with procedure, sir. I understand, sir. No, Mr. Vice President, it was an interesting conversation. I hate to admit it sir, we may have been a little out of our depth. That's very kind of you to put it that way, sir. Yes, sir, we'll be happy to do that."

With that he handed the phone back. The agents, for all their perfect conditioning and hatefully low body fat count, were drenched from head to toe.

"Sir, if we've offended you, please accept our apology. From the files we knew that you held a high position in a couple of administrations some years ago, that you had financial successes when you were young then devoted yourself to public service, mostly as an unpaid advisor on finance and foreign affairs. It seems that your problems began when you were quoted as saying that you were apolitical. This damaged your credibility so you resigned because the media said that you shouldn't work in the highest levels of the government in which you served. Of course our system of government depends on succeeding in politics to become elected and re-elected. When your name popped up on the guest list, it probably automatically triggered a review alert. Since you've been rather incommunicado for the last decade one thing led to another which electronically initiated the full blown vetting which led us here today."

"What else did they find? I traded with Cuban fishermen, dollars for fish and that I recently hosted a former Soviet deputy premiere and his buddies on a sail from Cuba to Bermuda."

"Well, yes. We have aerial and satellite surveillance and confirmation photos identifying the Blue Ghost's many trips to Cuba and sailing her waters unchallenged by the Cuban navy. With all the blow-up over Guantanamo Bay recently, you can imagine the concern over your unrestricted visits there. The 'company' identified the Russians, including the former deputy premiere, as having been KGB operatives at the highest level in the former Soviet Union. Again, more concern if you see what I mean. Two of them are now assigned to the Russian Embassy in Washington and spend their summer weekends near here in Cambridge. You are so fraught with potential international malfeasance, that you've become a text book case for every training regimen we offer. You've got the CIA, FBI and now us chasing our tails."

"Well, now what do you think?"

"I think our energy and resources could be better spent but

it took this incident to prove it. When someone like you gets all the bad boxes checked on top-secret security reviews, it's worthy of pursuit. Will you tell Johnson and me what you really think happened back then?"

"Firstly, do you think Cuba is going to attack us with all those 1958 Ford Fairlanes? Next, those Russians used to be my enemies, now they are my friends. Remember, 'Trust but Verify'? The world is shrinking. If we're to live in peace, dialogue, diplomacy and friendship are the wide avenues to that destination. On resigning, there's not too much to tell that you won't find annotated in my file. Despite my relationship with the Vice President, we were rather fierce business rivals after I got out of the service. I was young then and saw how much money his company was making, so I started my own little shop doing the exact same thing. They weren't happy with me back then. He became successful and went into politics. He's a sharp guy whom people underestimate or overestimate but he always uses this to his own best advantage. Later, I wrote books, started my own consulting company, then think tank and lectured. We came into the same government through eerily opposite paths yet wound up working together in some areas. I've never voted. I don't believe in 'one man, one vote' democracy which I have always believed to be fruitless, contrived, and fraudulent and controlled by the media. I consider myself a good American though."

"Sir, no one ever said that you were unpatriotic. Your war record, medals, honors and service will speak to that and you pay a ton in taxes. The amount you donate to charities is beyond exemplary. You're right; it was your 'non-political' views, if that's a phrase. The press at the time cited every word you ever used in your books, op-ed columns and articles to attempt to force you out but you knew that. It's a little strange. You were completely vetted back then. The administration knew you well. They knew all this before they asked you to come into the government."

"No Harlow, the media came after me to embarrass the administration. Controversy sells. They could have cared less about me. They'd known everything I'd said and written long before I took up my advisory post in the government. Then they just howled at my political aversions during a slow anti administration month. Companies won't pay for advertising unless a network or newspaper has large number of viewers and no one is interested in good news, muck-raking and such sells better. The government must have been doing something right for a long time for the media to plaster my well known bio and personal views on every front page and network news. After all, by calling me un-American it taints my employer. It's curious that it broke with every network and paper on the exact same day though. Six weeks after I left, editorials and Sunday morning news shows were somewhat applauding my right to such a stance on political parties to which The Constitution makes no reference; 'free speech' and all that. I turned down an appearance on national shows whose producers promised a non-antagonistic, supportive interview. Doesn't it bother you that some of our people despise other Americans who hold different even opposite political opinions from their own? This is akin to racism, even worse. In fact those who hold such head strong, violent political views are racist inside. On the surface they're hypocrites. It's true for both sides too. They start attacking the opposition the day after the other party is elected even though the next primary is over four years away. If their party wins they begin to campaign again in mid November after the election and before the inauguration in January for the next election four years hence. No matter what they try to accomplish for the country, advisors are there to make sure that it's political 'hay' and not political damage. I've felt like this since high school and I wrote and said that long before I was asked to work as an advisor and resigned. By the way, the president refused to accept my first resignation. I've been taking it easy ever since; taking it easy as best I can is the best thing for me."

"Well, what kind of government do you think we should have?"

"Mr. Harlow, I'd like to try 'Benevolent Despotism' for a while."

"Of course you'd be the despot."

"No, I think you, Mr. Harlow, is whom we need. You're honest, trust worthy and have good sense of fair play. I already know you are brave and a good man so you and you only would appoint people you know are qualified and have the same qualities, someone like Johnson here. You are beholding to no one, your word is immediate law until you change it. A modern day Solomon if you will."

"Did you know the VP would call?"

"I put a call into his office as soon as I saw the suits hanging around the day before yesterday but I was as surprised as you were."

"'Abilene' is obviously an old code word loosely describing the situation you thought you were in. I can't agree with the descriptions you used for our superiors though. They've all had distinguished careers especially in the line of duty. Why did say you that and what's up with 'Papa'? What else don't you believe in?"

"I lose my temper less often than before but I was upset. I still can't quite control my emotions at times, neither can the VP but he's getting up there so he has to try harder. As you know I'm ten years younger. You'll have to look 'Papa' up. It's not an alias since I didn't give it to myself. Where's your Latin? I try to be easy on people and not pry. My hope is that they'll be easy on me too. Besides being apolitical, I'm an agnostic, anti-social and a theoretical but non practicing sexist. In spite of that, I keep up on world affairs; attend different churches some Sundays, sometimes for the choir, sometimes for the sermon. I like people who are likeable and know that women are more intelligent than men. My beliefs derive from experience and are not trivially acquired. I've held most of them for more than half my life. I'm not invited to as many vibrant events as I would like because of that."

"Do you have any other rules about your boat?"

"Yes I do, no women under thirty-five or over forty-five."

"Well, no wonder you're alone."

"I may be alone but I'm never lonely."

❖ ❖ ❖ ⛵ ❖ ❖ ❖

Queen Anne's Princess

As the German made maroon sedan crunched its way up the circular driveway, Emily pinched the shear tulle-like curtain aside to glimpse down at the two younger women through the sun drenched windshield. Her former students arrived from Timonium on time. The stately woman couldn't decide if she had erred by inviting them again so soon after their last visit. She welcomed the company, especially in the form of two worldly women who admired and praised her. She could always take a lot of that. Her lone company throughout the year came from invited authors, Hanks, the retired waterman who now served her as gardener, handyman, chauffer and general factotum and her next door neighbor, Hannah, an African American widow who shared a regal, statuesque beauty with Emily.

Unless one knew for sure, the women in their mid seventies were easily imagined to be younger by two decades. Their two

Georgian homes erected by the same builder in the nineteenth century showed distinct similarities yet appeared unique. Centreville counted many houses whose owners had renewed and restored these classically designed homes and even with route # 213 running through the county seat, the town happily knew some anonymity. Most traffic just passed through.

Emily's father had been a scion of the county's more prosperous families. His people had reigned and been a force in local politics for two centuries. That's the way it was. The people who paid most of the county taxes ruled. The family businesses encompassed all conceivable revenue of the times including steamship service from all major ports along the Bay to and from Baltimore. Her father, reared in the family tradition of rough individualism, thought his only child should not be tempted by inheriting his rugged and cut throat companies and gently directed her to the arts and academic life. At the end of his life all his going concerns found buyers and he neatly tied all his assets up in cash, bonds and insurance for his daughter.

Besides the liquid assets, she retained her childhood and current residence in Centreville and a summer home on the Chester. The sprawling acreage which the family once oversaw there had been lessened by a few thousand acres with the condensation of material properties. Her father left fifty acres on the water with the house and these were acclaimed to be the best fifty of the lot. An architectural jewel with incomparable views down and across the river, Emily found numerous invitations from leading periodicals and magazines on her mantle to 'do a story with photographs' about the historical old homestead a few miles up from the mouth of the Chester. She randomly obliged depending upon the correctness, propriety and taste of the publisher. No feature on her private residence in town had been allowed. When interviewed, the occasions were always scheduled in the garden of the summer house at mid morning with the Chester as a backdrop.

"Well, you're certainly dolled up enough for these girls. Then again I can't imagine you throwing on cotton dress and sandals to greet company. It is the week after Labor Day. Don't you think silk is still warm especially during the day?"

"Oh Hannah, you know this old frock. I could roll it up in the palm of my hand it's so light."

"Are you ever going to speak American English? I mean it's perfectly fine for our conversations and chats but you practice it everywhere, even at the crab houses. Some of those poor servers can't even translate your response to their greetings. You say dear for expensive, lachrymose for sad and bonny for fine."

Her neighbor had taken the well worn tiled path from her own kitchen through their common English garden gate and up the back stairs to the dressing room adjacent to Emily's bedroom adorned with pictures of the English royal family and stood erectly with her head critically tilted as she apprised her friend. She hadn't knocked or cleared her throat. The two women spoke while Emily kept peering through the window; Hannah stood just inside the door.

"Firstly, my dearest, one doesn't practice the Queen's English, one executes and participates in it. Secondly, I attended a public, which means very private, school and university in England so I won't apologize or soften anything which gave me such a wonderful education."

"So you've said before but the paradox shouts incredulity. You won't have crabs that aren't cooked to order. If they come to the table in less than twenty minutes, you send them back. Only unwashed oysters in their own liquor are good enough for you to cook with. Sure, your higher education abroad refined you but you can crab and fish with the best of them. It's like you're two different people. You sail like an old tar and have published six novels, two of which have been made into terrible movies. You haven't written anything in years. Besides gardening, your only recreation now is receiving former students, editors and other literati who clap you on the back for being the very good writer you once were. I'm not calling you a 'has been' but lately you only write a few reviews, articles and letters. Now these two country club, forty something sycophants are here for the second time in nine months."

"Hannah, I've always said it's better to be a 'has been' than a 'never was.'"

"What's on the agenda this time? I guess we'll take them to the summer house which they love so much. They'll sit on the veranda after dinner and say how magical the sunset makes the river with its beams dancing on the Chester. I like them both for their goodness but I'm worried about you needing the prolific verbal caressing you seem to invite. Of course Deidra will insist again that she intends to write as soon as her youngest gets out of college. She'd have a hard time writing a grocery list."

"I would guess you're right in part. You enjoy the company as well and you know I'm not easily flattered. We both see the point of it. It's our contact with the outer world. I feel as we grow older the company lends enthusiasm to our lives, don't you? After Hanks shows them to their rooms, we'll meet them on the back portico for refreshments as usual. I do believe you may still be able to learn quite a deal from me."

"I meant what's the plan when we go down to the summer house. You're right. I could learn from you but I think I already know how to drink."

"Very droll I'm sure. I write and correspond in the morning then have my 'elevenses', usually a chilled bourbon and soda. I occupy myself intelligently and diligently the rest of the day until I announce 'Happy Hour' at four-thirty. You should know, you're here most afternoons. I take my two G and Ts as a sign that it's the end of the work a day world even if I don't toil much anymore. Besides the Queen has two G and Ts every afternoon as well. If it's good enough for a great sovereign, it's good enough for me. We always have wine with dinner. It's agreed, is it not, that well made wine not only aids in digestion but has other medicinal advantages as well. We rarely finish a bottle or have the last of the decanter. Drinking, my dear, is pouring pitchers of disgusting draft beer down one's gullet while sitting in beer joint like a sot."

"How about having a Coke instead of beer with crabs? That would be a start. We could start moderating with that."

"Lord save us, crabs without beer! This is heresy. We live in the garden spot in the region known as 'the land of pleasant living.' I'll forgive you your trespass and consider it venial and excusable. Let's pretend to no memory of 'crabs sans beer.' Sometimes I wonder what kind of Christian you are."

"The kind without a guilty liver. So what's up tomorrow?"

"We retreat to the river house after breakfast and a garden stroll. Hanks has prepared all the rooms and brought the motor craft up from Queenstown. We'll lunch at Harris's on Kent

Narrows, crab cakes and spiced shrimp. By the time we arrive back we'll have a light supper and sit on the back portico and watch the dancing sun beams transcend into moon beams."

"Now who's being droll? Why is it a motor craft instead of a boat? Why don't we go down and greet them at the top of the steps on the porch like normal people?"

"That's just not how it's done. Hanks will show them to their rooms so they may refresh themselves and change. They will have a chance to relax and anticipate their hostesses."

"Lord, I wonder how many 'outfits' and shoes they've brought this time. Hanks could hardly manage their cases last time. He's getting too old to be toting that luggage up and down these stairs. They probably have a case with Frankincense and Mur for you."

"Oh posh, that was in the winter when the clothes would have been heavier but I do see. We shan't make him carry them again. Deidra and Sally golf and exercise at some gymnasium so I assume they're rather fit enough. It just isn't proper to entertain house guests and make them manage for themselves."

"Emily, this isn't Buckingham Palace."

"Oh, that it were!"

"I just don't like strangers gazing at you as if you were a loon when you speak."

"You're so caring to indulge me. I do love vocabulary and idioms which are apropos, well placed and well spoken. You are the only person in the world with whom I may banter and chat with in the English I love so well. If it weren't for you my words would never be alive in speech, only on the printed page where, unread, they atrophy and die. Besides, you enjoy our exchanges as much as I. You have the thrill of the verbal joust and, at the same time, the joy of giving me the devil about being a word snob. We are fortunate. Do you know where the word 'snob' comes from? Allow me to say anyway. At Oxford and Cambridge only the children of royalty and the issue from the clergy were allowed to matriculate. Most classes were in Latin. Centuries later, the bourgeois were permitted to attend because their fathers were richer than many of impoverished royals. This nouveau riche crowd, deemed the third estate, was the wealthy merchants of the empire and tried and demanded to be treated on par with those who theretofore had looked down their noses at them. So when their sons were finally allowed to attend, the master who called the roll each day before class would mark the attendance sheet. Pierce-Jones, Viscount or Abingdon, Lord were duly checked off as being present. When Mr. Cooper was recognized as in attendance, the master thought it his duty to record after the check mark to note 'sine nobilitas' which means without nobility. Later they abbreviated that in the rolls to 's.nob.', then to 'snob', hence the etymology of the word. The definition however derived from the fact that these students were the ones who went around town acting as if they were better than anyone else. The royal's and the bishop's children always felt very comfortable in their own skin. They didn't act conceitedly. They had been reared in that elegant, genteel air of centuries of sophistication. They didn't have to prove that they were better than everyone else, they knew it. It was the pretenders to an upper station who desired to let the word know how very special they were. In a word, they became 'snobs.'"

"Well, it's still like that today. People who have to prove something to others haven't proved to themselves yet. So what else is on the schedule?"

"Thursday Hanks will take us up to Rockhall for crabs at 'Waterman's.' I just love sitting on the deck picking crabs overlooking the marina. You know, that's where father directed all his enterprises from."

"Don't you mean 'from where father directed all his enterprises.'"

"Shame on you, now you mock me."

"Well, I thought one should never end a sentence with a preposition."

"Our Sir Winston Churchill changed that imperative forever when he said, 'that is one grammatical rule up with which I shall not put.'"

"Oh Em, you do delight me. I guess if you had been a boy your father would have reared you to follow in his footsteps."

"No, I don't believe so. Father was blackguard and rather coarse. He once told me that the nature of the times demanded that a man be more unscrupulous than his foes and competitors to remain successful. He told me that everyone wanted what he had. It seems to have been ruthless and trying times. I believe he had a kind heart but, except for me, was not presented opportunities to manifest his goodness. I know him mostly through the letters which he wrote to me while I was away at school and our brief summers together. He wrote beautifully. Even when I came to the summer house on vacation he would pen a lovely note each morning. It always wished me a fruitful day and he anticipated with pent up delight our supper and evening together."

"Was he the one who taught you to eat crabs? I've never seen anyone get as much from one of those Jimmies as you. For all your refinement, a dozen steamed crabs in front of you look like they've been scrubbed with a scouring pad and run through the dishwasher when you're done with them."

"Most people just want the jumbo lump meat from the backfin. Once you clean, prepare and pick the crab to eat, there are so many delicacies. The mustard, especially inside the vacant shell and the sweet, tasty part inside the knuckles are not to be discarded. I've seen crab eaters leave enough good meat to make two nice sized crab cakes. Yes, he showed me and those were the happiest days of my childhood. Father owned a thriving seafood business as well which shipped to Philadelphia, Baltimore and New York. He would warn anyone who would listen that they were over fishing the Bay but times were so hard and there was no science or any idea that we'd have the problems we faced later. Watermen were getting a nickel then ten cents a crab, before that, a dollar a bushel. Father thought that if we were to harvest and eat this delicacy of all delicacies, we should not waste any of it. You know Hannah, I've had guests from Sweden, who eat seafood seven days a week, tell me that our steamed crabs are the most delicious seafood they've ever eaten. I've had similar comments from Japanese chefs and Alaskan fishermen."

"You weave a story well. I believe it is an art but your passion for the Bay and its way of life is the core of your gift. We are both fortunate to be able to give and donate to help restore these waters."

"Yes, and the oysters are promising with the experiments down on the Great Wicomico River in Virginia. Underwater scientists have seen the oysters filtering, actually blowing 'smoke rings.' If we can put men on the moon, we can revive the Bay."

"I'll allow you to call it a water craft anytime. If you wish to call the radio a wireless so be it. When I moved next door to you, I thought you reclusive, aloof, even conceited. Now you're my neighbor and friend. You have enriched my life. I love you."

"Love is all you need."

"Who said that?"

"Me, John Lennon and Sir Paul McCartney."

"Of course, he will always be Sir Paul to you from now on."

"How could it be otherwise? He's a knight of the realm."

"Most English ex-pats think we're spoiled by birthright and I can see why Americans take a lot for granted. Do you know what the Brits said about the G.I.'s in England during the war? 'They're over paid, they're over sexed and they're over here.'"

"I never said I liked the English, just England."

"You are more American than most. Don't your people trace themselves back to the sixteen hundreds? Your last name is Smith just like the island. You've never said much about your mother. She was probably a Tilghman."

"My dear, your last name is Smith as well."

"That was the name of the people who owned us down in Saint Mary's county. That's why I'm a Catholic as well. When my family crossed the Bay to the Eastern Shore before the Civil War they had a harder time than most. It was difficult to be picked up by land owners. That's why my great grandfather started working on the water. You have to remember the Eastern Shore was a hotbed of the Confederacy. Even up in Baltimore Union Armies held the city under siege because of all the southern sympathizers. There weren't many Catholics of color in those days over here either, still aren't."

"I never knew my mother. My father hired au pair girls from Genève to rear me. When I was teenager, a rather nasty girl with oily skin came up to me at a picnic and shouted in a most vile screed that my mother had been a prostitute plying her trade on one of the steamships in my fathers company. Later I begged my friends to ask their parents if they knew anything about the story. I could tell by their embarrassed demeanor when I queried them later that there was more validity than fiction in the denials with which they assured me."

"So did your father ever mention her?"

"No, he only told me that my mother died very young not long after I was born. That was nineteen thirty-four. He did assure me that he was my father but there are no family photographs, no record of any marriage and no mention of anyone who ever knew her."

"Did you believe him?"

"My father never told a lie in his life. Besides, I resemble him in so many ways; not just the way I hold a crab knife. I believe my instincts for literature, writing and reading I derive from him. The books in the library have been there since I was a child. He died on the front veranda of the river house one evening. He had just finished his Southern Comfort. He wore his seersucker suit with his knit tie loose. The New York Times crossword was perfectly and neatly filled out in ink on the end table. No, he may have been a crusty, no nonsense business man but other talents were his as well. My father had a sense of royalty which I have never been able to capture or portray successfully in my work. The French put it well, 'je ne sais quoi.'"

"I think we say 'that certain something' or 'it' I also think there are personal circumstances in your life that appear in your first novel."

"Oh Hannah you are more than just clever. Why must I always put a flare of verbal panache, a hint of exotic mystery in my speech? You are correct. What must some people think of me at times? However all authors should write what they know about or at least try. A hint of imagination and wistfulness help, if they have any."

"People probably think of you as I think of the British 'expats' over here."

"Oh, how horrible I must seem. You have more of knowledge of Britain than I believed you possessed. How did you come by it?"

"Let's go back to your life's experience woven through your novels. What part is your imagination, what part is your life and what is your wistfulness, or is it just plain wishing?"

"Well, maybe we should save that for another day. The girls will be ready soon. We should be prepared to receive them."

"Nonsense, they'll be another fifteen minutes. All the changing and primping they do makes me think they're not quite so confident in themselves."

"You're very well read so I don't have to tell you that more than a bit of Jane Austen has crept into my work. I so admired her writing when I was a teenager that I knew her theme of the rich, landed master would fall in love the pretty maiden, despite his attempts not to, would influence my writing. I've tried to disguise it but I fear the critics and readers readily recognized a lonely woman, as Jane was, who rather wished she could be the heroine she created on paper. My simple twist, which became borne from truth, manifested itself from the fact that I was the young, wealthy, landed heiress whom the Lotharios sought. Jane, not altogether impoverished and well educated in art, music and other refinements of her middle class station, had a sprinkling of gentry in her part of the English countryside. When I turned sixteen in nineteen fifty, most of the men had returned from the war and gone back to work. Around here, you see, that meant on the water. There were a few boys to choose from but they seemed rather fey or undistinguished. The others were hardscrabble ruffians of whom father would have never approved and at the time I agreed. I'm sure father shipped me off to school in England to refine me in order to meet a husband in Philadelphia or New York. The ideal here at that time of course centered on the connections one had at The Naval Academy; to marry an officer and be stationed abroad with one's husband. When I returned home for the summer my few friends recounted the balls and galas in Annapolis. They begged me to convince father to send me to college readably accessible to the Academy. I did have two dates with a midshipman. Both were chaperoned and we were doubled but on the second one he had us slip away. We attended a party of sorts in town where he tried to get me intoxicated with several sloe gin fizzes. On the way back to my friend's home he tried to make out with me. At first I was rather amenable. The evening shone brightly and we ducked into the front yard of large house within a block of the academy. No one was home and we settled on the front porch and sat on a hammock, I'm afraid it ended all terribly though. He immediately put his hand up my dress. When I pushed it away with both my hands, his hands were all over my breasts. I insisted we retire to our company at the soiree at my friend's home, only down the street."

"Did he oblige?"

"Yes of course, with a plethora of apologies."

"Well that doesn't sound like it ended so 'terribly.'"

"Oh, that's not what I meant. He was mortally wounded in Korea as a Marine captain. I received two letters from him after we were informed of his death. Looking back, I now realize that people in the prime of their lives, especially young men are more sexually driven than at any other time. When one is in the best physical shape of their lives, their mental acuity at an apex, the natural urge to propagate overwhelms them at times. In those days restraint was practiced more than any generation since."

"You're saying that a horny boy is driven by an innate sense to further the human race and not a need and desire to just 'have it off' as you would say."

"Certainly dear, they don't see it that way of course but at the bottom of it the men are driven and controlled by a wellspring of male hormones. Thusly laden, I find it remarkable how they even function at their jobs during the day. The world should attach more consideration to the plight of civilized men over the past four hundred years."

"Good Lord, I've been your neighbor and friend for over year and you surprise me almost daily. I've read your novels and really cannot discern which part is you and which derives from that fervent brain and imagination of yours. If authors only write what they know about, how do you come by these plots and characters? Your life seems a reclusive paradox. No one lives and loves the Bay, the Chester, an idyllic Chesapeake way of life more than you. You pretend to all things English yet I don't think you'd visit again. In fact you haven't alluded to any trip or vacation you've made recently. All your stories set in the U.K. are from years, even decades ago. Is it a double life or a dual personality? You are a woman of the Eastern Shore, a

Marylander and an American. Really Emily, why allude to another life when you have a perfectly contented existence here. Why the lust to be two halves of a single person? When others don't know you well, they mistake you for a snob. What are dinner plans for tonight?"

"I'll serve my crab casserole and salad with the last of the summer's tomatoes, cucumbers, the June garlic and my secret vinaigrette. I think some Chablis grand cru should do nicely don't you?"

"I'd like to have your recipe for that."

"My secret must forever remain forever a secret. Otherwise it loses its cachet as a secret."

"I'm not speaking of your dressing. Anyone knows that it's white wine vinegar, ground black pepper, a dash of garlic and fresh lemon juice and Dijonaise mustard. You think because you sprinkle in little crushed red peppers at the end that it's some mystery."

"Did you refer to my renowned vinaigrette as dressing? I've confounded master chefs with that recipe. It's not written down anywhere. How could you know?"

"I know because I have a tongue. Your admirers were neither masters nor chefs. Or, they had the good grace not to displease their hostess. No, I meant the casserole. Secret vinaigrette indeed."

"Oh that's no secret. Father showed me. We had a cook and other staff but when it came to crabs or oysters he prepared the meals. I should not tell you for being so cruel about my secret 'dressing.'"

"Oh pooh, Em. What's the recipe."

"Simply chop a red pepper, three ribs of celery, a small onion and some parsley. Sautee the pepper, celery and onion in butter but don't brown them. Layer a pound of jumbo lump crab meat on top of crushed Ritz crackers in a buttered baking dish with the veggies and two thinly sliced hard boiled eggs. Dilute a can of mushroom soup with milk and pour over the creation. Sprinkle cracker crumbs on top and bake. Simple."

"Good lord, you're just like every other person who doesn't cook from recipes. At what temperature and how long should it bake?"

"I'd say about three hundred and fifty degrees. I think about twenty to thirty minutes. I just take it out when it starts to bubble up. It serves four nicely don't you think?"

"I think it's the most delicious crab dish I've ever tasted."

"How charmingly nice of you to say, thank you. Hannah you know so much more about me than I do you. I believe it's terribly unseemly to pry or even ask about personal matters. My curiosity has been at a peak these last months. You are a mystery and you must how my artistic temperament is provoked by such enigmas, especially with someone whom I've grown so genuinely fond. Your demeanor and your bearing lead me to imagine scenarios I know aren't factual. Before we go down please oblige me to soothe this longing I have."

"Yes I wonder myself how the fates and the furies threw us together like this. We were born in the same year only miles apart but travelled such divergent paths. About the time that you arrived home from England, I arrived there. The late fifties were difficult times for people of color in this country, obviously. I met a boy, a genius, in Baltimore at a dance club. He was from St. Mary's County as well. I was about three years older than he. He had a quartet that played jazz, jive, and dance music at all black honkey-tonks from Atlantic City to the segregated beaches on the Bay, mostly around Annapolis. He could play every instrument including drums and not just pieces in the group, every instrument. He never had a lesson except from other musicians while they were jamming. From guitar he taught himself the violin and cello. When our eyes caught each other during a break they spoke to each other as if he and I had nothing to do with it. He bought me a coke and asked if he could see me after the dance. I told him 'no.' I wouldn't stay out that late so we arranged to meet on Sunday. Of course I fell in love with him. He was so handsome in a boyish sort of way. All the women adored him and he could have had his pick, not just of some, but all. We were married in New York and left for Europe the following week. We both had grown tired of the prejudice and the bad pay. We had both heard that France and England were less prejudicial than America. We were wrong. There was no racism there at all. It was if we had changed our color to white. No one even blinked at the fact that we were not only colored but Americans as well. If anything, James enjoyed great success immediately because of his talent. As you know the arts have always flourished in Europe. One is not black or white, only an artist."

"How long were you there?"

"Twenty-two years."

"Did you ever miss America? Weren't you ever homesick?"

"What we thankfully missed or didn't get to experience were the assassinations of President Kennedy, Dr. King and Robert Kennedy. There is crime everywhere but there is less violent crime abroad. We never had the children we wanted so badly and that gave us the freedom to spend our lives as we wished.

We made wonderful friends, had a nice home and travelled Europe when we could afford it. James had steady work as a studio musician, played on some Beatle tracks among others. We lived first hand the swinging sixties, were invited to all the parties and had a great life there. We were older than most of James's friends and never got caught up in the drug scene. We both knew of the horrors and tragedies of addiction before we left. For us it was easy 'to just say no.'"

"Why did you come back to America?"

"I don't know exactly. The luxury and excitement of travel, moving to a foreign land, the 'wanderlust' had always been our common bond except for our love. One day we decided to come back here as if it were an exotic land, a challenge to see what would happen. We moved to New York where James taught music, bought a home in Connecticut and knew we had made the correct decision. James died two years ago pruning the roses in our garden."

"Why here, why come back here?"

"I've seen a lot places, mostly Europe, north Africa and the middle east. We were good savers and I could live any where I choose. I'm from the Eastern Shore. I was born here, married here and wish to die here. This is the garden spot of whole world to me. This is my Eden as it yours. I looked for a year before settling next door. My father worked on the water. My mother was a crab picker at a packing plant. They had a hard life. My father always said that it would be a hard life anywhere so it may as well be on the Chesapeake."

"What an absolutely and stunningly romantic life you've led. I feel such a fool bantering on about 'jolly olde England.' You know it far better than I."

"Em, there isn't a street in London upon which I have not trodden. I've walked from Earl's Court to Stepny and from Hampstead to Brixton. I've travelled from Cornwall to the Orkney Islands."

"I'm absolutely amazed. Do you think England is part of our bond?"

"I think Queen Anne's County, the Chester and the Bay are our bond. England is now just a moderate conversation piece. Would you live anywhere else? I doubt it."

"There is no doubt. Your generosity in time and financial support of restoration and preservation came to my attention only because I chair a local group which aids the larger organizations. I never asked what you did while your husband worked."

"I painted seascapes, landscapes, dogs and horses. I never painted people."

"Are those paintings which hang in your house your work?"

"Most are, yes. I stopped painting when James died. It's just as well. As you know the talent and all that implies is a finite pool for any artist. I'd like to paint Shelly and Keats though with your permission. Why is Shelly the Golden Retriever and Keats the Bay Retriever? Is there a poetic connection that I'm missing?"

"No, not really, I was in my cups when I named them. Then the next day I couldn't remember which one I had named which so I called them both Shelly and both Keats until they wound up who they are today. Have you ever painted Elizabeth? I don't think I've seen her on the walls. So your English influence is not without explanation now. You named her after the Queen."

"No, I named her after my mother. I've done a small genre

painting of her which sits on my nightstand."

"Where did you get her? Is she a breed?"

"I don't know. I rescued her from the pound. She's definitely a terrier. I believe she's mostly an Airedale but who knows."

"Well, I made up a little ditty about her as she was barking at the FedEx man yesterday. Would you like to hear it?"

"We're both honored."

"Wait until you hear it first."

'She has one eye blue, one eye brown

One ear up, one ear down

And a chopped off tail that won't go 'round

She runs and chases without losing a breath

But only with food may you befriend fair Elizabeth.'

"Isn't that corny? But it popped into my little brain while she jousted at the fence with the intruder."

"That sums her up perfectly. Words are your thing, Em."

"I would have thought that one of us would have Welch Corgis like the Queen."

"Oh now Hannah, you hit the nail on the head earlier when you said that this is our home, the Eastern Shore. This is the land of Retrievers, Labs and of course Terriers."

"There are no dogs in your novels. Is there a reason? The excellent way you write, I would have thought that you could have woven a few furry friends into some of the characters."

"You are astute. This will sound potty to you and it is. It's impossible for me to create a dog of fiction because by doing so I give it a name, a home, a life span. Just because the pet doesn't die in the novel, he or she would have lived in my mind just like all my characters. You see, to me all the thirty something personas I created fifty years ago grow old in my mind. I came to be fond of them even if they were villainous. They would all be in their upper eighties now, not the swashbuckling, debonair men or the beautiful women who still exist on the page fixed in time and ageless. Many from my first books would have passed away by now. I can do that to people but I could never do that to a dog."

"Emily, I can't quite express the elation of knowing you this closely for the rest of my life. It's like living next door to a princess."

"I hear Elizabeth greeting the girls on the veranda. They were quicker than normal this time."

"Em?"

"Yes Hannah?"

"That is a beautiful frock."

❖ ❖ ❖ ⛵ ❖ ❖ ❖

The Point Lookout Lookout

As soon as the campers were bedded down for the afternoon rest period, Rick and Smiley headed for the beach past the latrine and the archery range. Both counselors knew that their charges didn't need a rest in the middle of the afternoon; ten and eleven year old boys have as much spunk as any age group in all humanity. In fact, the main reason for this two hour hiatus was to keep these over-charged gremlins out of the mid summer sun which would crisply burn their ill shaped heads and bodies to the unhealthy reddened shade found on a Campbell's Soup can. The brilliant, hot summer afternoons near the southern tip of Saint Mary's county warmly pleaded for serenity and shade but not by this ragamuffin horde of unbound energy. Another more pragmatic cause for this forced incarceration sprang from the merciful intention of the camp director to relieve his teenage camp staff for a few hours each day from their monstrous little waifs. Eight buildings held two cabins each separated by a smaller two cot room assigned to the support staff. Four buildings were located north of the mess hall and four south of it with one large latrine out back to accompany each side. The wood framed out-buildings held ten boys and their leader. The director, a retired army lifer, could only guess, but he felt confident that without this enforced respite in the afternoon he would only return about seven kids a cabin to their families after a two week period. The World War Two veteran and former drill sergeant could easily calculate the numbers of strangulation, drowning and archery 'accidents' caused by his employees were he not to enforce a rest period for the boys and the mandatory break the counselors must take away from their charges. One cabin leader would serve as the proctor for the day and check on all sixteen cabin while the other fifteen counselors were free to participate in any activity available to them except there were none. Thirteen practiced passing, punting and running on the large athletic field in the center of the camp. Any ruckus from within a cabin would bring a harshly laced tirade from this unlucky policeman for the afternoon. Although this duty only fell upon him and his co-workers once every sixteen days, by the end of the summer they started to dread their rota a week in advance.

The salary of two hundred and fifty dollars for the four two week periods was never a princely sum but in Nineteen Fifty-Eight it became a cherished position since most applicants thought they could get an early start at getting in shape for football practice which convened a week after camp ended. Summer jobs for seventeen and eighteen year old high schoolers were hard to come by, even rarer for girls. While a summer of abstinence from swilling draft beer and being hounded by their parents were a trade-off, these semi-Neanderthals were hired partly because they possessed the talent and size to intimidate and threaten boys many times diminutive to them.

The summer camp had been a generous and forward thinking brainchild of a successful businessman man who had been reared in poor, working class conditions in the inner city and recalled the ennui of his summer days in the morbidly hot and humid alleys of Washington D.C. He had purchased the land, hundreds of remotely graceful and serene acres along the Chesapeake just north of Point Lookout where the Potomac washes into the Bay.

The width of the Chesapeake at that juncture seems as endless as the ocean and its expanse promised to lead to remote lands that the campers could but imagine. In fact the distance from the Point Lookout to the eastern shore measures the widest part of the Bay. The philanthropic man had his workers put up the buildings and he subsidized half the fee of twenty dollars for each boy for the two weeks. The average cost per child amounted to at least twice that sum. Many parents could not afford even the ten spot and some kids came with little more than what they had on their backs, an old towel, a threadbare single sheet and no pillowcase or blanket. This poorer than poor contingent received a subsidy of the essentials like a toothbrush, bed linen and swim trunks. The kindly benefactor became a great hero to the boys when he paid visits during the summer but even he was not spared their wise cracking insults and continuous ribbings they reserved for no one, especially each other. They would surround the portly old man with the bald pate and demand money, make bitter complaints about their treatment and demand the entire staff be jailed for feigned offences known not even to the most un-civilized countries of the day. The elderly benefactor, who had not forgotten his roots, could give as well as he could get. When one of the young rotters who had him surrounded shrilled,

'When I grow up I'm gonna start a company and put you out of business, Pops.' The old man laughed back, 'Dumbo, your ears are too big to be that smart.'

The uproar of laughter turned the boys' barbs toward the big eared kid but only for about thirty seconds until some other wit hollered,

'Oh, Yeah! Tommy's gonna grow into them ears, I don't know what you're gonna do about that bald spot, Pops.'

Another roar and the 'jone-ing', the boy's verb for this recreation, continued. The exchange was the only form of reverence known to them. This substituted for their thanks and appreciation they had never been taught to express. Only Dickensian London had known such youthful rabble.

Rick and Smiley were the only counselors who did not revile their charges; Rick, because he had the sole distinction of being a former camper for four summers and Smiley, because there wasn't anyone or anything he disliked, hence his nickname. There are those in life who are blessed with, followed by and exude an aura of a good mood. Smiley, whose christened name was James Joyce Ryan, bore that gift with the same grace which made him unaffected by it. Rick, at sixteen, had held the best staff position in camp, head mess boy, before being appointed the counselor of cabin eight next to seven, Smiley's billet. This promotion came only a week after the beginning of camp and at his age made him the youngest counselor in the camp's seven year history. Eddie Jones, the former leader of cabin eight, it seems, had received the steamiest of heavily perfumed letters in a hot pink silken envelope with scarlet lipstick kisses smacked everywhere except over the address line. The exotic epistle arrived five days into the first period in mid June. The foolhardy eighteen year old boy put off perusing its contents until an hour after lights-out.

Under the privacy of his blanket with the aid of his mandatory flashlight the eruptible Eddie settled in to enjoy this posted erotica. The sender put no return address on the envelope but there could be no doubt that his steady, known as Melissa the 'Kissa' for her constantly smooching the beloved Eddie, had posted the supposed love letter. The exact contents were only known to the authoress, Eddie, the director and the camp nurse, who pried the missive from the sex- stricken teenager as the local rescue squad wheeled the stretcher into the ambulance.

The gist of the note, rumor spread, indicated not so much the love and affection the girlfriend held for her departed boyfriend but a rather detailed and encyclopedic litany of every lewd, lascivious and erotic act she or they would be performing were he only back in town with her. Upon re-reading the letter for the twelfth time in twelve minutes, poor Eddie's genitals grew to such a swollen state, that the intended personal act of pleasuring himself for some needed relief became impossible because of the slightest contact his hand had with the affected area. That first squeezed grip drew such an apoplexy of morbid pain that the entire camp was awakened with his screaming prayer for relief or death. At the first shriek every camper in number eight awoke and sprinted out the door. Most were rounded up in the woods hours later and a few only came forward at dawn. These kids were tough but rather feared an unknown which would make someone who played high school football, was three times their size and almost twice their age writhe in such agony. Surely, if fortunate, they might later experience a similar proposal but be closer in proximity to their temptress and not miles away on a desolate peninsula sharing a room with ten kids. After the medics had tended to the disabled Eddie they rushed him to the hospital at Patuxent Naval Air Station in Lexington Park where the Navy doctors were well up on the treatment of this singular and peculiarly male ailment. The director had seen this in his regiments but commented that Eddie's ballooned scrotum had to be prized as the largest and the color bluer than the largest blue 'Jimmy' ever caught in the camp's boating lagoon. Released from the sick bay, Eddie returned to town and tried his hand at selling paint for the summer.

Smiley had learned a lot from Rick by the time the last period began in mid August. Running a group of ten boys of that ilk took some insight and although Smiley had a natural ability for it, there were tricks and nuances for being a glorified baby sitter in these circumstances. Since Rick had been a camper, he knew the ins and outs of dealing with everyday life and how to adjust to the senior staff, the cooks, the boredom and especially the boys. Already popular with the staff, Rick's esteem grew for the good job he had done since taking over cabin eight in such short notice. On the face of it, the director would have never hired him as a counselor that spring because of his age. The previous summer Rick had worked in the kitchen as an ordinary mess boy at seventy-five dollars, then promoted to head kitchen boy this season at one hundred per season. Finally, due to the plight of the unfortunate Eddie, his unsavory mail and his testicular ailment, Rick became a full fledged counselor whose employment now became guaranteed for the next two summers. Smiley it seems only applied for the job at the last minute and jumped ahead of twenty applicants for the last position because the director and senior staff easily identified his abundance of calm abilities, quiet confidence and overall charming demeanor. The fact that Smiley had been an 'All City' athlete in football and baseball the previous school year and handled that fame and notoriety with such an inconsequential attitude and air of un-false humility, gave great weight to his hiring. One other unmentioned attribute added to his persona. If the Greek god Adonis had sought the same position and the job went to the more handsome, Adonis may well have had to spend his summer as a paint salesman too. It's not often that kids are struck by the good looks of other guys but Smiley was the exception that proved the rule. If they weren't aware of how good looking he was, they could scarcely avoid the praising comments of their sisters, mothers and girlfriends who almost genuflected at the sound of his name and swooned unashamedly in his presence.

Smiley acknowledged to Rick after a friendship grew out of necessity and proximity that he had no intention of taking this job but for the threatening way a ferocious man had come to Smiley's home, stood in the middle of the street at three A.M. yelling at Smiley's house in the most violent manner. Swearing that that his intention was to break Smiley's handsome face were he ever to be seen with his sister Cynthia again, Smiley decided to abruptly seek after employment. This job would remove him from the vicinity, indeed the entire city and its environs. He found it not only necessary to stay out of harm's way but harm itself. He must avoid the fiery temper of the brother but also, with secrecy and distance, the absorbed college soph, Cynthia, who it seems would rather stalk him all hours of the day and night. When lightly quizzed by Rick, Smiley did admit to heavy petting sessions and protected sex once with the girl but only after she pretended to an attempt of hurling herself off the Calvert Street Bridge onto the crags of Rock Creek Park below. The threat of death, especially his own, led Smiley to this oasis with room, board and spending money for his second attempt at having a successful senior year and graduating the following June.

Walking down the unspoiled beach toward the inlet of the lagoon, which served as the boating area for the campers and geographically labeled a creek on maps, Rick waded into the breaking waves. As Smiley kept walking, Rick swam parallel to him helped by a current. After reaching the inlet to the southerly lagoon, they crossed on foot, careful of the abundant crabs that swam in and out of the thirty yard wide entrance according to the tide. They could catch two dozen jumbos with only a net in five minutes or less. For four days the boys had brought whatever material they could scrounge to 'decorate' a duck blind built on the southern edge of the lagoon and the beach. Smiley's real girl friend was coming Sunday, visitor's day for staff and campers. Smiley had arranged a tryst with her and she would be prepared with the necessities, beer, and sandwiches. Smiley would provide two condoms.

"Look, Rick I really appreciate this. I haven't been with a girl all summer. Joanne is so good looking. Wait 'til you meet her."

"Smiley, I don't want to meet her. I want to meet a girl like her. I'm helping you fix up this little love shack and going to sit in a dinghy to keep kids and parents from bringing a row boat too close so you two can do it in a duck blind. What's in it for me again?"

"You're helping a friend and as soon as we get back home I'm going to turn you onto a girl and not that nut, Cynthia.

Someone you'll like. I just don't know who yet. I think we should nail this canvas on top instead of trusting it to just lay there. You know, in case a storm comes up the Bay."

"Jesus Smiley, why don't we put in an ice box, toilet and phone? You got a foot of straw covered by that blue tarp, covered by two sheets and two pillows with cases for Christ's sake. When we get back, don't give me any crap about not being able to find any girl good enough, I'll take anybody. When the hunters find this in the fall they're not going to know what happened."

"You sure do cuss a lot, Rick. Is that so you'll sound older? Is it the same reason you won't let people call you Ricky? Hey, you're a good looking kid but you look too young. That's why you can't get any girl to go with you. Girls are funny. They like guys who are mature looking and can give them a secure feeling. If a guy has a job or is in college so they will be able to get a job is even better. If you have a car and a job, you're in. Your day will come. The difference is I was shaving when I was fourteen and you don't even shave yet. Besides you're sixteen but look twelve."

"That's crap, Smiley, I don't cuss too much and I don't want anybody older than eighteen or nineteen."

"You're right about that. The world revolves around eighteen year olds girls. When I first masturbated it was to an eighteen year old girl. I fell in love with an eighteen year old girl when I was fourteen. I kissed my first eighteen year old when I was sixteen and had sex with her on my seventeenth birthday but by then she was almost nineteen. When I get out of school next year I'll be nineteen and a half and am going to marry Joanne who is the same age."

"Married? Are you nuts? You can have almost any girl in

town. You've told me how they camp out in your yard and show up everywhere you go even with your family."

"Yeah, I've had all that. That's why I want to marry Joanne. I just want one girl to be with all the time."

"What about college and the scholarships to play ball you're going to get? Think about all the girls there are in college."

"Yeah, I've played enough ball. Been playing since I was ten. No, we're getting married. She's going to work next week on Capitol Hill as a secretary or something and I'm going to join the electrician's union when I graduate. Her uncle has his own construction company and is going to get me in. After the apprenticeship, it's good money."

"Smiley, electricians are what guys become from my side of town. Isn't your father a doctor and your mother a librarian? Don't you think they'd want you to go to college, or at least give it a try?"

"Yeah, but that's their gig. I got my own. Besides, mom's only a volunteer at the library."

"Do you know you have an annoying way of saying 'Yeah' a lot?"

"Yeah, I know. It is a habit."

So it went until the most beautiful day of the summer appeared on that visitor's day. No one could be sure that it was still August. Small clouds wafted by slowly. The flag pole in front of the mess hall resisted the light whipping of The Colors and various banners gave the pole a pleasant slapping sound so you could not only feel the breeze but hear it. On the Bay an old freighter chugged northward, her bow trying to catch the smoke from her two stacks blown over her by a trailing wind. Rick's sense of dread to this point evaporated in the warm sun. He was impatient to see this girl and waited in front of the cabin while Smiley was posing for pictures and showing a camper's family the beach. As the cars pulled through the gate, he kept an eye out for a '56 white Chevy with a baby blue convertible top, Joanne's high school graduation gift. Serenely cruising through the gate and ignoring the newly posted '10 MPH' signs, Joanne pulled up to the front of cabin '7.' A cloud of dust and dirt followed the most beautiful girl or woman Rick had ever seen in person or in the movies. She slowly untied a white silk scarf around her neck then peeled the gossamer fabric, back from her thick black, silky hair. Pulling the rear view mirror toward her, she decided no freshening or repair was needed and slid out the door. Seeing him staring at her, she smilingly and sweetly walked up to the gawking teen.

"Hi. I'm Joanne. You must be Rick. Would you give me a hand putting the top up, it might rain?"

Her baby blue silk dress almost matched the convertible top. "Smiley told you about me?"

"Oh, he's an inveterate letter writer. Don't tell him I said so though. I can only imagine what he told you about me."

Unable to form any answer, he stared at the ground because he didn't know what 'inveterate' meant. Misreading his awkwardness for politeness of not mentioning anything personal, she continued.

"Do you think it will rain today?", now her turn at uneasiness.

"No, it hasn't rained all summer. He'll be here in a minute; he's with a couple of his campers and their parents."

"Mr. Personality. People like him. I think he'd make a great father once he grows up himself, don't you?"

"He seems pretty grown-up to me now."

"Oh, you mean the sports and his mature looks and that confidence. That's good if you have it but I fear its only surface stuff. Did he tell you what he did last year? After football season he told his parents he was going to Europe the day after Christmas for three months."

"No, I don't think I heard that one. I know he has to repeat his senior year. I thought he flunked."

"Flunked? He gets straight 'As', another one of his gifts. His parents bought him an airline ticket, stuffed thousands of dollars of traveler's checks in his jacket and drove him to New York to catch the plane. He came home with all of the money they gave him and some very nice but curious jewelry, a ring, a watch and gold cigarette lighter. He doesn't even smoke. Then he was dismayed when the school wouldn't let him return to class and play baseball right away."

"That does sound like him."

"Are you coming with us on the picnic? I've brought plenty of food."

"Me? No, he's taking you in a row boat to a really neat spot on the beach with great views of the Bay. See how blue the water looks today with those white caps."

"Blue is my favorite color."

The two lovers drove down to the boating area since the picnic basket would have been too unwieldy to carry even for Smiley. Following discreetly, Rick waited at the dock until they reached the mouth of the lagoon and watched as Smiley beached the boat and helped Joanne off. Rick then pulled one of the two dinghies from the boat shed which had a sign on it marked in Smiley's hand 'Do Not Use. Under Repair.' Rick dragged the small craft to the water, turned her over and put her in. He loved the two little boats which only counselors and the boating director were allowed to use. The fine burnt orange shellacked interior wood, which so perfectly framed the inside deck and seat, made him feel almost nautical each time he oared her over the placid, sheltered waters. Lagoon sounded more exotic than creek to the kids. It was they who renamed it. The wide creek was full with every able boat afloat with campers and their families. Some were near the mouth and he propelled the well made small boat up there and lightly admonished them to stay clear of the inlet and under his breath, 'and whatever prurient and fornicating activities taking place just around the cove.' He pulled in the oars to enjoy as best he could some relaxing moments.

Visitor's day was over at three o' clock. It was now one-thirty. Smiley had another hour. As Rick leaned back just to doze, the tranquility, breeze and beauty brought him sleep. As he rested his head on the knob of the bow, an unusual rustle on the dinghy's underside broke his spell. Looking aft he noticed a rather large piece of drift wood float past at an alarming pace.

He'd been in this part of the world every summer for the past six years and he recognized this harbinger. In the quickest instant the sky went from blue to black. The light breeze had strengthened to stormy winds. White caps which could be seen earlier in the middle of the Bay now heaved themselves closer to the inlet. The dinghy bobbed furiously so that no part of her bottom ever touched the water at the same time. A mountain of crashing waves battered the beach. The first strike came right over where he knew the Point No Point Lighthouse to be. The bolt widened to the width of a football field and grew in light, color and size as it struck downward. The simultaneous thunder clap shook the entire lagoon like an earthquake. The rain came in sheets. Because of the tempest wind, the walls of water came from no particular but every direction. Between the gusts of downpour, he could see that most of the boats were in or almost in and make out the staff pulling the rest of the would-be sailors onto the dock. The counselors and staff had actually practiced emergency drills so thorough was the director and his military ways. All would be rounded up and herded into the Mess Hall using the taller flag poll far enough away as a lightening rod.

So concerned for the boaters, Rick had temporarily forgotten Smiley and Joanne. He never thought that he could possibly forget her until Smiley's boat sailed by the dinghy almost crashing into his port side. The self propelled, larger boat made it back to the dock area in a matter of minutes, usually a ten minute row, and crashed bow first into the pier. Pulling hard against the rush of the choppy tide, Rick oared to the south side where the blind was located. The dinghy began to take on water and he barely reached the brackish, marshy shore line. As he turned her over and secured her well into the woods, he yelled out Smiley's name but the din and gale of the storm brought back his shouts to him in an echo.

No easy path would take him to the blind. He lifted a downed tree limb to hold in front of his head to prevent all the wispy branches and prickly vines from slapping and cutting his drenched face. If they were to cut his eye or eyes he knew it would be impossible to find his way. He attempted to blaze a trail since he thought he may have to return the same way. As he trudged through the overgrown density, the thought occurred to him that no one had ever set foot on this ground ever, ever. When he reached them, he became aware of just how close he was to the blind; in distance. It had taken him twenty minutes to go sixty yards. A concerned but calm Joanne sat under the blue tarp used for the conjugal bed. Smiley, as unflappable as ever, had made a sort of tepee for them. He crouched next to her and was drinking a Budweiser. The canvas roof had caved in on them from the abundance of water.

While Rick didn't know exactly what to find, he was happy they seemed O.K. and that Joanne had her dress on. Her hair stuck to the side of her face and the long streams of black make-up that had run down her cheeks had faded and almost washed away leaving only grey out lines below her eyes. Smiley on the other hand looked like he could have gone to a party by simply putting on a dry shirt. For a moment no one spoke. Finally the older boy lifted up and said,

"Come on, get under here with us."

"Why Smiley, are you afraid I'll get wet? We've got to get back! We can't have somebody else round up our kids for us. We've got to be at our table in the mess hall with them. I've got a plan."

"What plan? We'll jump in the boat in a bit and with this rushing tide we'll be back in a minute. This will die down soon right?"

Rick was hushed. He stared at Smiley who wanted him so badly to agree with him.

"The boat washed away, didn't it? That's why you came out here; to get us."

When Joanne said this, a slight quiver came up in her voice that Rick heard but knew Smiley didn't. The older boy knew the boat must have washed back away in that churning torrent because he had only beached it but didn't want to upset the already frightened girl. He told her they could wait out the violent thunderstorm.

"You make it to the dinghy. I've made a path. It's not that far. Bring it back here. You're strong. I couldn't make this far. Take Joanne back in it. Take the car back to the cabins. Do a head-count. Get them into the mess hall if they aren't there already. The storm's coming from the south. I can swim straight out and let the tide push me north up across the mouth of the creek. I can't swim the lagoon and take a chance of getting washed down in that muck on the bottom. The beach is under water all the way to Lexington Park but there's that little stretch of incline up to the corn field just on the north side. Come and get me the with the car at the top of the incline. Use the tractor road that separates the field. You won't get stuck. The road is covered with years of husks. I've seen these storms. If they circulate and hover, they can last for hours. We've got to get back. I'm the best swimmer the camp has ever had, I can make it."

When the struggle to get the dinghy up to the blind was over, Smiley put Joanne on the small plank in the back and took Rick by the arm.

"Yeah, I've been thinking about it. You're going to drown, Rick. It's a great plan but you got it backwards. You're taking her back and picking me up at the corn field. You're right, we got to get back."

By now the force of the storm prevented even Smiley from standing up straight. Shouting at the top of their lungs at close range, the pounding surf and thunder made their voices nearly inaudible.

"I know you're a great swimmer, the best I've seen, but that's been in calm weather and easy water. This is not a question of swimming. It's a question of who's going to get across that inlet. The answer to that question is 'me.' It would be dangerous for you and not for me. This may be the only thing I've ever done for somebody other than myself. See you in twenty minutes."

After finding all twenty kids safe, more than half with their parents in the mess hall, Rick bolted out of the large structure. He had told the director almost the truth about needing to pick up Smiley with the car. They were both in big trouble and he knew it but getting Smiley back put all other thoughts from his mind. As he left he heard the nurse trying to lead the wet crowd of children and adults in a sing-song as the mess boys served everyone hot chocolate and Graham crackers. While the two teens waited in the car for any sign of Smiley, she broke the nervous silence.

"Did he tell you he wants to marry me?"

"Yes."

"He says we can get an apartment. He wants to become an electrician. He lives in world of his own. When extraordinary people like Smiley come along, it's they who must adjust to us. We're incapable of understanding them. He wanted to propose to me in the blind and then make love. I may be the only person in the world who really knows and understands him and that's what he loves."

"What did you tell him?"

"I told him the truth as he would expect me to."

"The truth about what?"

"We weren't going to get married or make love, he wasn't going to be an electrician and he was going to college, probably where his father went. I told him it was his attempt to just be normal. He wrote me a lot about you, never talks about himself, only other people. He said he liked you because you were normal and special at the same time. He said you said you looked after your kids and he liked that. He said you had a lot of ordinary things, problems going on in your life that he never had to deal with. He learned something from you."

"I won't be looking out for any more kids next year, not after this. If he's not here in a minute I've got to go down to the beach."

"What's that? It looks like my picnic basket. Is that him?"

When they reached him, he was laying down on his back and breathing heavily at the top of soaked grassy ramp Rick had described.

"I'll tell you two, I've done some wild things in my life but that had to be the top. When you left I had a great idea. I thought about using the basket like a preserver. I put my arms through the handles and headed straight out. You were right Rick, straight out and it washed me up the Bay, then I paddled left and the waves washed me right to shore. The hunters will get some free beer in November. Rick, you would have made it just as easy with or without the basket. Are the kids O.K? I bet the director is mad. Where's the car. I'm beat."

Since there was only one week left in the last session of the summer, the two were severely reprimanded and justly so but kept on during the final days. Their salaries would be halved when they received their checks in September by mail. This was another well deserved punishment. Neither would be welcome on the grounds again. Few words passed between them those last days but a few knowing smiles and nods were exchanged.

Besides, Smiley was always smiling. It was too soon after the fact to talk about the events of Sunday. Rick didn't know what was on Smiley's mind. He had only one recurring thought on his own; Smiley was right, he surely would have drowned but Smiley had told him differently in front of Joanne. On Wednesday Rick got a letter. In all the years as camper, busboy and now counselor he had never received a letter or a postcard. The envelope was pale blue.

> Dearest Rick,
> I told you that my favorite color was blue. I now have another reason I love your eyes. They're warm and sensitive and mean well.
> I start work next Monday. Please call me at home. F.E.3-6868
> I'll pick you up.
> Love at least 'til then and longer.
> Yours,
> Joanne
> XXX OOO

❖ ❖ ❖ ⚓ ❖ ❖ ❖

CHESAPEAKE BAY RECIPES

Solomons' Widow
Crab Balls

2	lbs jumbo lump crab meat
2	egg yolks
2	tbls mayonnaise
2	tbls brown mustard
2	dashes Worcestershire sauce
4	finely ground toasted pieces whole grain bread crumbs

Mix gently with fingers keeping the crab lumps intact as well as possible. Pull from the mixture a portion larger than a golf ball but smaller than a hardball. Twist the tops to dull point and sprinkle the tops with J.O. spice. Place on buttered broiling dish. Set broiler at 400°F. Watch 'til toasty brown.Usually 5-10 minutes. *Serves 2-8*

The Road to Hampton Roads
Oysters Rockefeller

24	oysters in shells
2	tsps chopped parsley
2	tsps chopped raw spinach
1	tsp chopped tarragon
1	tsp chopped chervil
1	tsp chopped basil
2	tsps chopped chives
	salt and pepper
1	cup of breadcrumbs
1	stick of butter

Shuck oysters, keeping as much of the oyster liquor as possible in the bottom shell. Discard top shells. Place shells on a baking sheet with one oyster in each shell. Sprinkle thickly with the parsley, spinach, tarragon, chervil, basil and chives. Season with salt and pepper. Cover the tops with breadcumbs and dot with butter. Bake at 450°F for 5 minutes. Serve hot. *Serves 6*

Annapolis Annie
Grilled Soft-Shelled Crabs

4	tbls deli-style mustard
3	tbls melted butter
8	prime soft-shelled crabs, dressed

Preheat the grill. Mix mustard with enough melted butter to make a liquid paste. Brush on the crabs. Place on grill for 2 minutes on each side. Serve immediately. *Serves 4*

Tennis Ball Beach
Steamed Blue Crabs

5-6	dozen large Bay blue crabs
1	cup beer
1	cup water
1	cup Worcestershire sauce

Sprinkle crabs liberally with J.O. Spice or Old Bay seasoning. Steam 25 minutes until bright red. *Serves a crowd*

The Choptank Chum*p
Oyster Fritters

1	pint oysters and liquor	Drain oysters, reserving the liquor.
½	cup evaporated milk	Combine all except oil into a large
1	cup pancake mix	bowl. Mix into a thick batter. Heat the
2	tbls corn meal	oil in a large frying pan. Drop battered
1	tsp salt	oysters into the hot oil. Fry until golden
	black pepper	brown on one side 1-2 minutes. Turn
	cooking oil	over and brown the other side.
		Serves 12

A Day on The Bay
Miles River Crab Soup

1	pint oysters and liquor	Simmer the onions lightly in butter.
2	tbls butter	Add crabmeat and heat through. Add
2	small onions, chopped fine	flour and follow with hot milk; stir
1	lb crabmeat	slowly and let boil for about 10
2	tbls flour	minutes. Add corn, lima beans, and
4	cups hot milk	seasoning; let simmer another 10
1	cup grated corn, cooked	minutes. Add cream. Before serving,
1	cup small lima beans, cooked	add sherry; reheat. *Serves 6*
	salt and black pepper	
1	tsp Worcestershire sauce	
1	cup cream	
4	tbls sherry	

Easton Summertime
Crab Salad

1	lb jumbo lump crab meat
6	spears white asparagus, chopped
2	fresh shredded carrots
½	cup diced pimento
1	cup sliced zucchini
	white wine
	lemon juice
	Dijon mustard
	fresh ground pepper

Peel carrots into curls. Cut asparagus into thirds. Steam all vegetables al dente. Mix mustard with white wine, lemon juice and ground pepper. Pour sauce on veggies. Add cold crab meat. Top with a sprinkling of J.O. Spice or Old Bay seasoning. *Serves 3-4*

Queen Anne's Princess
Crab Casserole

	Ritz cracker crumbs
1	lb jumbo lumb crab meat
1	red pepper, chopped
3	celery ribs, chopped
1	small onion, chopped
2	hard-boiled eggs, thinly sliced
1	can cream of mushroom soup
	milk
	parsley

Sautée red pepper, celery, onion in butter but don't brown them. Add parsely. Cover bottom of a buttered baking dish with Ritz cracker crumbs. Layer with crab meat, sautéed veggies and hard boiled eggs. Dilute mushroom soup with milk and pour over ingredients. Cover with layer of cracker crumbs. Bake at 350°F until bubbly for 20-25 minutes. *Serves 4*

The Point Lookout Lookout
Crab Cakes

1	lb lump crab meat
½	cup whole wheat bread crumbs
⅓	cup chopped onion
⅓	cup chopped celery
2	tbls mayonnaise
1	tbls minced fresh basil
1	tsp deli-style mustard
2	tsp Worcestershire sauce
⅛	tsp cayenne pepper
1	egg, beaten

Combine into a bowl. Divide the mixture into 4 large patties. Cover and chill for 1 hour. Coat a large skillet with cooking spray and heat until hot. Add patties and cook 5 minutes on each side or until golden brown. *Serves 4*